The Draconia Novels

Dragon Riders
The Egg That Wouldn't Hatch
Dragon Magic
The Dragon Who Chooses Twice
The Girl, the Gryphon, and the Dragon
The Mage's Dilemma
The Seer's Challenge
The Dragon and the Unicorn

The Dragonwind Novels

The Fox, the Stag, and the Dragon
Dragon Sanctuary
Dragons, Mages, and Magic

DRAGONS, MAGES, AND MAGIC

DRAGONS, MAGES, AND MAGIC

by

DAPHNE ASHLING PURPUS

ISBN: 978-1-7326402-2-1

Purpus Publishing, Vashon, WA

Even the smallest person can change the course of the future.

J. R. R. *Tolkien*

TABLE OF CONTENTS

List of Characters and Places

Aloysius: Estrea's most learned historian. He lives in the palace, in the turret where the archives are stored.

Basil: A mage who works with Rastan.

Bergamen: A nearly translucent light-purple, very small, newly hatched dragon with one damaged wing.

Blossom: A pink female dragon who is the best healer among the dragons.

Claude: A nonmage who grew up in the slums of the capital but now runs a number of scams. He's acquired a lot of the property that was confiscated from the four noblemen when they lost their standing after working for The Wraith.

Clyde: Brother of Claude. He's a mage, like their father, Durkin.

Criseda: A turquoise female dragon who serves as the dragon ambassador to humans and who works closely with Ty.

Dr. Brunfeld: The palace doctor, a white-haired, stooped-shouldered, elderly man with kind eyes.

Dragonwind: Ty's village, which is near the dragons' aerie.

Driselda: A large emerald-green dragon who is the historian for the aerie.

Durkin: A mage living in the capital. He's Claude and Clyde's father.

Edward: The smallest fox in the fox communication network.

Elfrida: A retired schoolteacher living in Dragonwind.

Eloise: Gorst's wife. She stays in the village when Gorst leaves.

Ernest: Nearly-three-year-old son of King Bertram and Queen Elicia.

Esme: A fifteen-year-old girl with magical gifts who was abused and tortured by her parents but now lives with Martha, who is her guardian. She is short and thin, with short brown hair and kind brown eyes.

Estrea: The nation ruled by King Bertram, which contains the village of Dragonwind.

Felicity: A palace maid.

Foster: A male green dragon.

Foxy: A black cat who lives with Ty.

Gorst: Along with a group of friends, he is a troublemaker who doesn't want anyone different, especially magical, living in the village.

Gwen: A young serving girl at the palace.

Harriet: Five-year-old twin daughter of King Bertram and Queen Elicia.

Harvey: The lead fox in the capital for the fox communication network now that Rupert lives in Dragonwind.

Hazel: Five-year-old twin daughter of King Bertram and Queen Elicia.

Henry: The steward at King Bertram's Palace.

Irene: A mother living with her daughter, Jennie, in the slums of the capital. She is in her early thirties, with long blond hair and blue eyes.

Jasper: A fifteen-year-old boy with black hair, dark complexion, and wiry build, small for his age, with a lot of magical talent. His father is the mage Rastan, and his mother disappeared when he was five.

Jeb: The gamekeeper and warden for the forests around Dragonwind. He and Ty are best friends. He is tall, taller than Ty, and has a medium build, dark brown hair, and brown eyes.

Jennie: The six-year-old daughter of Irene. She has long blond pigtails and blue eyes.

King Bertram: King of Estrea. He is in his late thirties and is tall and well built, with dark-brown hair and brown eyes. He is married to Queen Elicia. They have three sons and two daughters.

Kyle: A former hermit who now lives with Martha. He is tall and solidly built, with hazel eyes, nearly white hair, and a bushy gray beard. He is in his midfifties.

Lance: The eleven-year-old son of King Bertram and Queen Elicia.

Martha: A short, heavyset woman in her midfifties, with gray hair and eyes and a kind, plump face. She raised Ty after his parents were killed, and now she's raising Esme.

Naomi: Paul's mother, also rescued from the mining villages and now living in Dragonwind.

Oscar: A young orange male dragon with yellow wings.

Paul: A seven-year-old boy who was rescued from the mining villages. He's telepathic and very close to Wilhelmina.

Queen Elicia: A tall, slender woman with red hair and blue eyes; she's thirty-four years old and married to King Bertram. They have three boys and two daughters.

Rastan: A powerful and vengeful mage. He is tall, with broad shoulders, athletic but slightly heavyset build, light-brown hair, and blue eyes. He is able to control weather, and is telekinetic, and strongly telepathic. Jasper is his son.

Raymond: The seventeen-year-old son of King Bertram and Queen Elicia, the eldest and Bertram's heir.

Ribendi: An ancient predecessor race of dragons from which the current dragons developed centuries ago.

Roland: Dr. Brunfeld's assistant. He's a tall young man with short brown hair and brown eyes.

Rupert: A red male fox now living in Dragonwind. He runs the fox telepathic network between King Bertram in the palace and Ty in Dragonwind. He's friends with Samantha and Esme.

Samantha: A gray telepathic squirrel who's a friend of both Rupert and Esme.

Sapphire: A bluish-purple female dragon. She is the leader for all the dragons.

Simion: The captain of the palace guards.

Tobias: A very ancient philosopher who studied the legends and stories of Estrea.

Ty: A nineteen-year-old who governs Dragonwind and also serves as an ambassador for King Bertram when needed. He has both telepathic and healing powers. His parents were killed when he was six, by which time he knew he was truly a boy born into a girl's body. After he caught those who killed his parents and exposed the crimes of the king's half brother, the dragons granted him the body that he should have been born with.

Ventus: A large blue dragon who mated with Windsong. Bergamen is their son.

Wilhelmina: A large moose who is the strongest telepath on the planet.

Wilson: A refugee from one of the small mining villages along with his wife, Selena, and son, Ralph. He is the lead carpenter in Dragonwind.

Windsong: A nearly white dragon, translucent in tone, with just a hint of purple. She and Ventus are the parents of Bergamen.

CHAPTER 1

CAPTURE

Jasper was freezing. He and his father, Rastan the mage, were hiding near the top of the mountain, watching the dragon sitting on her nest. Rastan, a tall man with broad shoulders, an athletic but slightly heavyset build, light-brown hair, and blue eyes, was determined to capture and kill dragons, and he'd chosen to start with a pair of dragons who'd left the dragons' aerie to live on their own.

Jasper was ashamed of how proud Rastan was that he'd managed to kill the male, a magnificent blue dragon named Ventus, three days ago when he came upon the pair in the mountains. The pair fought hard to defend their egg. Ventus tried to knock Rastan off the cliff where the nest was situated, but Rastan shot him with a poisoned arrow and then watched as the poison took hold of the blue dragon, causing him to writhe in pain before he finally succumbed. Rastan found joy in watching the dragon die, but Jasper just felt sick and horrified.

The female, who was a translucent white with just a hint of purple, let out an earsplitting cry, grabbed the egg, and flew away before Rastan could take another shot. It took Rastan three days to find her new nesting place.

Jasper really hated helping his father. He thought dragons were beautiful. His only memory of his mother, who had disappeared when he was just five years old, was of the stories about dragons that she used to tell him. She told him ancient legends that had been passed down in her family that said dragons had helped humans a long time ago, until humans betrayed them. She even sang about them, and he was totally enchanted. He wanted to learn more about dragons, but he hadn't been able to after his mother left. His father had laughed at his mother's stories and said that humans had hunted dragons for food until they all ran away to the aerie.

Now he just had his father, who was cruel and who demanded total obedience. If his father told him to do something, well, then he had to do it. He might be fifteen, and thus nearly an adult, but he was small for his age, and his father had been cruel to him ever since he was born. Jasper had his mother's dark complexion, black hair, and a wiry build. He was small for his age, which made Rastan angry as well, and Jasper just couldn't stand up to him. If he disobeyed, he was beaten. If he didn't obey fast enough, he was beaten. If he made a mistake, he was beaten. Jasper lived in fear, unable to defend himself. He just tried to do what he was told and to stay out of his father's reach. His father said that he needed to be hard on Jasper to toughen him up because the world was an unfriendly place, full of dangers, and Jasper was too kind to survive in such a world.

Rastan whispered to Jasper, "Get the net up into the trees, and make sure it is over the dragon. But don't you dare make any noise or alarm her. Do you hear me? Don't mess up."

"Yes, Father," said Jasper as he crawled over to the net they had brought. He slung the net over his shoulder and began to climb the tree nearest to the dragon. He moved very carefully and slowly. This was all so wrong, but he knew his father would whip him if he didn't obey.

Jasper crawled out along the branch that reached above the dragon's nest. His father spoke to him telepathically, saying, *Be careful! Open out the net, and let me know when you're in position.*

Jasper did as his father instructed and then said, also telepathically, *I'm in position.*

His father commanded, *Throw the net over the dragon. I'll help to guide it magically.*

Jasper knew that his father could have used his telekinesis, even though that wasn't his strongest magical power, to do the entire operation. However, he wanted to force Jasper to help with his evil plan. Jasper threw the net out over the beautiful dragon, and sure enough, his father took magical control

2

of the net, ensuring that it landed on the lovely creature, trapping her and her egg.

Then his father raced up to the dragon, who was thrashing, trying to get the net off herself. Rastan had a metal chain that he snapped onto the dragon's front right leg. He then took the other end of the chain, which had a spike fastened to it, and drove the spike into a nearby rock using a hammer. Just to make sure, he took another identical chain and snapped it onto the dragon's left rear leg, driving the chain's spike into another rock.

Jasper climbed down from the tree and walked slowly over to his father and the dragon. As Jasper looked at the beautiful dragon, whose translucent scales seemed to shimmer in the afternoon sun, their eyes met, and then he was startled when she spoke telepathically to him.

Don't worry. Your father can't hear us. I know you didn't want to do this. We'll talk more later, but try not to worry.

Jasper just nodded as a tear rolled down his cheek. He couldn't believe that this magnificent creature had been trapped, and even more unbelievably, that she was worried about him. No one worried about him. No one cared about him. Even his mother had left him. And why not? He wasn't even brave enough to warn the dragon. He was too afraid of his father.

His father yelled at him, "Jasper, get over here! Help me take this net off her. She can't go anywhere now. She's mine. And grab her egg. She won't need that anymore."

"What?" exclaimed Jasper. "She needs to keep it warm so it will hatch."

"Hatch!" said his father. "I'm trying to get rid of the dragons, not make more of them."

His father kicked at the egg, and it rolled toward the edge of the cliff they were on. Jasper couldn't help himself. He ran after the egg and caught it just as it was about to crash off the cliff. Thankfully, his father wasn't paying any attention to him by then. His father never paid attention to him unless he wanted to punish Jasper, but for once, Jasper was glad to be ignored. He gently cradled the egg in both hands before he placed the large egg into his backpack as he said, *I'll take good care of your egg.*

Thank you. My name is Windsong, and the egg you just saved holds my son, Bergamen. He's not quite ready to hatch, but I have been teaching him. Dragons can learn while they

3

are still in their eggs. We'll chat more later. Just know that I can shield you, so you're safe from your father.

Thanks, said Jasper, overwhelmed by the fact that even in her capture, she was trying to comfort him. He then helped his father remove the net.

"What are we going to feed her?" asked Jasper once the net was off Windsong.

"We aren't going to feed her anything or let her have any water. I'm going to watch her die and observe her efforts to save herself. Dragons are supposed to be so all-powerful. Let's see what she can do. You know that my grandfather gave me a mission before he died. I'm the first mage in our family since my great-great-grandfather, and my grandfather told me that it was my responsibility to take vengeance on the dragons who killed my ancestor, your ancestor, and stole our land. All this land," Rastan said as he waved his arms around, "used to be ours. I'm going to claim it no matter what. That means killing the dragons."

"But that's horrible," said Jasper, feeling sick to his stomach.

"Ha," said his father. "I plan to kill all the dragons. I need to know the best way to do that. As she weakens I'll invade her mind and force her to divulge the secrets of the dragons. I know they are telepathic, and I'll make her talk. I need to show people that I'm more powerful than those in the capital think. You know we can't be seen in the capital, that people hate you because of your mother and your dark skin. I need you to help me. So I can't just get rid of you. But when I prove how powerful I am by being able to kill dragons, then they'll have to accept me."

"Why? Dragons are magnificent creatures."

"They think they're more powerful than I am," said Rastan. "That's why I need to prove my power. Once I prove my power, we can live anywhere, and no one can attack us. Generations ago my family was important. They owned most of the land around here, and they were the strongest dragon hunters. We're going to be that powerful again. Don't you see that I'm doing this for you?"

"No, I don't. We don't need to live in the capital. We're doing fine on our own, aren't we?" asked Jasper. "Dragons don't bother us. They don't interact with most humans at all. They live in their aerie and have nothing to do with any humans, even the villagers in Dragonwind, the closest human village."

"These two left the aerie, and if we're not careful, more will leave in the future," said Rastan. "They're always around poking their noses where they don't belong. I'm going to get my family's land back again and rule over it. But first I need to get rid of the dragons. And you're going to help me."

Jasper looked down at the ground, saying nothing. He wondered just how he could defeat his father, but then he realized that his father was too strong for him. He certainly didn't believe that Rastan was doing all this to protect him. He just needed Jasper to cook and clean and make camp.

His father finished checking to be sure Windsong was secure and then said, "We're going home now, and you better have dinner ready soon."

Jasper followed his father down the mountain trail toward the cave they had found. It took nearly an hour to reach it. Jasper was exhausted, but he knew that he had to make a fire and then cook something for dinner. His father went into the cave and began making notes about the dragon.

Jasper started the fire in their firepit and then set to work trying to make a stew. He hated cooking, but if he didn't make dinner, then he'd go hungry. He'd learned that early on. If his father had to cook, then he cooked only for himself. He claimed that he did that to discipline Jasper and to teach him obedience.

By the time dinner was over, Jasper was absolutely exhausted. He had taken some of the coals from the fire and placed them around the dragon egg in a spot away from the cave where he hoped his father wouldn't find it. He really wanted to go back and check on Windsong, but he didn't think he could make the trek in the dark. He went to the spot in the cave where he'd put down his blanket and tried to go to sleep. He didn't know if she could hear him, but as he pulled his blanket over himself, he said, *Good night, Windsong.*

Good night, Jasper, she answered. *We'll talk tomorrow, I promise. I've checked on Bergamen in his egg, and he's doing fine. You gave him a warm, cozy spot. Thank you so much!*

I hate my father. I don't know why he has to do this. I'm so sorry.

This isn't your fault at all, said Windsong. *Just look after Bergamen.*

I will. I promise, said Jasper before he fell asleep.

CHAPTER 2

HATCHING

The next morning Jasper made breakfast, slicing bread and cheese, and handed a plate to his father. As Rastan ate, he said, "I'm going to spend the day trying to get that dragon to talk. I don't want you to get anywhere near her. You'll stay here in the camp. Chop wood for our fires, snare some rabbits and then dry the meat, and clean up. Have dinner ready when I return."

Jasper looked at his own plate, and suddenly he wasn't hungry anymore. That poor dragon. He wondered if there wasn't something he could do to make things better for her.

"Did you hear me, boy?" shouted Rastan.

"Yes," said Jasper.

"Well, just see that you do what I say," said Rastan as he stood, grabbed his pack of supplies, and left the camp.

As soon as Rastan was out of sight, Jasper grabbed a leather water pouch and filled it. Then he began to make his way toward Windsong's nest, being very careful to climb quietly and to stay out of his father's line of sight. He was much faster than his father, so he reached Windsong before his father arrived.

"Here's some water for you," Jasper said quietly when he reached Windsong.

You shouldn't have come, said Windsong.

7

I had to. I couldn't let you suffer alone, said Jasper. *I know I'm not good for anything, but I can't just stand by.*

What do you mean, you aren't good for anything? said Windsong. *I think you're very brave and clever.*

No, said Jasper. *I'm not. I'm clumsy and stupid and good for nothing. Just ask my father.*

Your father is an evil man, said Windsong. *He's a bully who can only feel powerful when he abuses others. Don't believe anything he says about you.*

Jasper poured more of the water into Windsong's mouth for her. *I'm sorry I can't do more for you.*

You are doing the most important job there is. You're looking after my son and protecting him. Listen to me. You can't help me. But you and Bergamen are going to change the world. It's vital that you two keep each other safe. Nothing else matters. I'll teach you as well as Bergamen, but you have to promise me not to take chances like this again.

But— began Jasper.

Windsong interrupted. *I'll explain more later, but you need to promise me not to try to help me, but to focus your energies on yourself and Bergamen. Also, you must do your best not to believe anything your father says. Can you do that for me? Promise!*

But...

Promise! commanded Windsong. *I know I'm expecting a lot from you, but you can do this.*

Jasper nodded just as he heard his father on the path.

Go now, said Windsong.

Jasper slipped into the bushes just as his father came into the clearing. "Well, you're not so high and mighty now, are you? You will tell me all about the dragons and reveal all their secrets to me."

As Rastan said this, he pulled out a long knife and approached Windsong. "Let's see if I can get some of the scales off of you."

Jasper slapped a hand over his mouth to keep himself from yelling out as he watched his father slide his knife under one of Windsong's lovely white scales.

Go, Jasper, said Windsong. *Don't look back. Keep Bergamen safe. He needs you, and you need him.*

8

Jasper turned and headed back down the path to the campsite. Tears ran down his cheeks. Why couldn't he stop his father? This was so very wrong.

▲

The next week was really hard for Jasper. He did keep his promise to Windsong as he looked after Bergamen, keeping the egg warm, turning it several times each day, and making sure it was hidden from his father. Windsong grew weaker and weaker. Jasper kept his promise to Windsong and didn't try to see her again. Every evening his father would gloat at dinner, obviously enjoying all the pain he was causing Windsong. He'd even strung a necklace with the scales he'd removed from her, and he took pleasure in showing it to Jasper.

"That's horribly cruel," said Jasper. "Why do you do that? Isn't it enough to starve her?"

"No, it isn't enough," said his father. "She's not letting me into her mind. She's not giving me the dragons' secrets."

"You're torturing her," said Jasper.

"So what?" answered his father. "She's just an animal, a stupid beast."

"You know the dragons are intelligent. You know they have their own magic. She's obviously smarter than you, because you can't make her do what you want."

Rastan stood up in a flash, stepped over the campfire to Jasper, and hit him hard across the face. "Don't you speak to me like that. I have all the power, and she will die. She may have some magic, but it's not as strong as my magic, and I'll prove it. No one will think dragons are strong when they're all dead. She will talk to me and let me know the dragon secrets. It's just a matter of time."

Jasper knew any further conversation was pointless, so he tried to ignore his father as he went about his chores. The only good thing Jasper could look forward to was his telepathic conversations with Windsong. She would talk with him whenever he was doing his chores and his father was away up the mountain.

You know that you've got a lot of magic of your own, don't you? Windsong said one afternoon.

Me? No, said Jasper. *I can talk to my father telepathically, although to be honest, I wish I couldn't, because he's always in my head and reading my mind. But I don't have magic.*

You do, actually, and it's strong magic. You'll discover that as you become an adult. Rastan knows about your power, and he pulls on it to enhance his own. He's stronger when you're nearby, but don't let him know I told you that. Meanwhile, I can try to teach you to block your father, if you want.

You can? That would be fantastic! said Jasper. For the next few days, Windsong taught Jasper to shield his thoughts. She showed him how to narrow the focus of his telepathy so that it was directed only to her. Then, amazingly, she showed him how to talk with Bergamen. That was the most wonderful thing Jasper had ever experienced.

I can talk to both of you, said Jasper one evening as he was getting ready for bed.

Bergamen said, *I like you. Do you like me?*

Yes, answered Jasper. *I can't wait until you hatch and I can meet you properly.*

It won't be long now, said Windsong. *I'm only waiting until Bergamen hatches before I leave.*

Leave? said Jasper in alarm.

She's going to become a true dragon spirit, said Bergamen, sadness in his thoughts.

But why? Can't you defeat my father, or escape? asked Jasper.

You have to understand, said Windsong. *Ventus and I left the aerie because we believed that dragons should live in this world along with everyone else and not separate themselves at the top of the mountain. Dragons keep themselves apart from everyone else and only act in this world when humans really mess things up, not just for themselves but for the planet and all other life forms.*

When Baron Geldsmith tried to take over the world, the dragons supported Ty in his bid to stop the baron. But they only did this after the baron gained a lot of power and threatened everything. They did not help Ty when the baron had Ty's parents killed when Ty was only six.

Later, when The Wraith was trying to control everything and everyone, they did not step in, even when The Wraith was kidnapping and enslaving children, forcing them to work in the mines and then collapsing the mines so that the children were killed. It wasn't until The

Wraith started to harm more than just humans, when he was gaining enough power to take over the world, that they assisted Ty and the others who were fighting him.

Ventus and I felt that things shouldn't have to get so absolutely horrible before dragons help. We are part of this world, and we need to serve it. So we left the aerie, and we were planning to work with Ty once Bergamen was born. But your father found us first, and he killed Ventus as Ventus was trying to protect me. Then he captured me and now is starving me. I can't go back to the dragons, and I really don't want to go on without Ventus.

There has to be a better way for the dragons to be in this world, and I'm counting on you and Bergamen to find it. You can trust Ty, and the dragons have advanced to the point where Sapphire, as leader, has allowed Criseda to be the dragon ambassador to the humans. It's a small start, and I hope it will continue, but I'm no longer up to the fight, she concluded.

You can't let my father win, said Jasper.

He won't, said Windsong. *I will never let him into my mind. I will not betray the dragons. I won't let him kill me. I'll just disappear one day. But the only way I can do that is to slide into the spirit world. Trust me. This is for the best, and I'll be with Ventus again. He slid into the spirit world before the poison could kill him. We'll be together again.*

Beginning with Bergamen and you, human-dragon relationships will shift radically. I know this, as I'm gifted with foresight. You two will form an unbreakable bond, and you will be the first dragon-human pair. Your lives will be challenging because you will be the first, and the first of anything is always new and not always received well. But your lives will also be exciting, and you will know that you'll never be alone. The two of you will be like a single entity, knowing each other's thoughts and feelings, working together as a team. I envy you this chance.

Jasper was quiet, and finally he said, *I've never had a friend.*

This will be so much more than friendship, but you'll discover that. And after the abuse you've suffered from your father, you deserve someone who loves and understands you. Bergamen will be that for you, just as you will be for him.

After a few minutes, Bergamen said, *When will I hatch? I want to meet Jasper… will I see you?*

Windsong was quiet and finally said, *I'm sorry, Bergamen, but no, you won't see me except in your mind. My plan is that as you are hatching, I will vanish to distract Rastan. Then comes your challenge. The two of you will have to escape and hide. This is actually the main reason I've been working with both of you on shielding your thoughts from others. I'm not sure if you're strong enough to keep Rastan out of your head, but you're going to have to try, and my goal is to distract Rastan long enough to give you a head start.*

Both Jasper and Bergamen were very quiet. They were each trying to process Windsong's words. Suddenly Jasper and Bergamen both gave telepathic gasps and then said at the same time, *I can feel you as a part of me!*

Windsong laughed and said, *I'm so happy. You two are still separate beings, but you're also a part of each other and always will be. Bergamen, you will hatch tomorrow. I've taught you all that I can, and I'm really sorry you'll never get to meet your father. He'd be so very proud of you, as am I. Now, this will be our last time to talk. Jasper, I must know: Do you know the way to the dragons' aerie? That's where you'll need to go.*

Yes, said Jasper, *but it's a long way. It's in the mountains above the village of Dragonwind. It will take me more than a day to walk it.*

I know, said Windsong, *and you'll need to feed Bergamen, as he'll be a new hatchling and therefore not able to help you. You'll need to carry him in your pack. He'll grow fast, but he'll still be very vulnerable for now.*

Jasper hesitated. *I know where lots of caves are between here and there, but then so does my father, and he's a really strong mage. I don't know if I can keep us safe.*

I have confidence in you, Jasper, and I've seen a vision of the two of you standing in front of Sapphire, so I know somehow you will do this, said Windsong.

I don't know, said Jasper hesitantly.

We can do this, Mom, said Bergamen. *I might be small and newly hatched, but I can help. I can help shield us and provide encouragement. I'll be strong, and we will do this. I'll make you proud of me, I promise.*

I know you both will, and I feel so lucky to be the one to teach you and explain about your bond. Now, both of you, get some rest. The next few days will be especially challenging, said Windsong.

Jasper crawled under his covers and tried to go to sleep. He had so much to think about, and now he shared Bergamen's thoughts as well. Finally, both of them slept.

In the morning Jasper's father told him to pack up the campsite, as they would be shifting their location that evening. Jasper knew better than to ask why. His father insisted that they change locations every week or so. Jasper hated the constant moving. This time, however, he realized it might work to his advantage.

After his father left to see how Windsong was doing, Jasper went to check on Bergamen's egg. Just as Windsong had said, the egg was rocking and had begun to crack. Within an hour, Bergamen had broken free. He was small, about the size of a puppy. But Jasper was worried when he saw that one of Bergamen's wings was broken. It was also much smaller than the other. And Jasper knew through their bond that the wing was really hurting Bergamen.

My wing broke when your father kicked my egg, said Bergamen. *I didn't want my mother to know. She would have just worried.*

I'm no healer, said Jasper. *I don't know what to do.*

Let's just get out of here. The dragons will know once we get to the aerie.

Jasper gathered all the food that he could. He was glad that he'd just dried a lot of meat, mostly rabbit, as he could feed that to Bergamen. He packed a few clothes, but only to provide a soft spot in the bag for Bergamen. He put on as many of his clothes as he could, because it was cold, and it would only get colder.

Once he'd packed, given Bergamen some dried meat, and settled the tiny dragon in his pack, he headed out. He scrambled down the path, away from where Windsong was chained up. He walked as quickly as he could.

The trail was tough. Jasper had to climb up hills and then back down again. There didn't seem to be any level ground where he could go faster. He stopped every hour to give Bergamen more food. The little dragon was being brave, but Jasper could feel he was in a lot of pain, and he couldn't eat much at one time.

Don't worry, said Bergamen. *I'm tougher than I look.*

I'm not sure about that, said Jasper.

At that moment both Bergamen and Jasper saw a vision of Windsong. She was standing, chained, in front of Rastan. They could hear Rastan taunting her. "Die, you foolish dragon, die! If you won't let me read your thoughts, then you are no use at all."

Windsong spread her wings and said, so that not only Rastan but Bergamen and Jasper could hear her telepathically, *You'll never kill me. Don't you realize you'll lose? Dragons have the ability to slip into the spirit realm, where they will live forever. You are a fool, a stupid fool.*

Before Rastan could respond, Windsong vanished, leaving the chains dangling from the rock.

Bergamen and Jasper looked at each other, and Bergamen said, *My mom is truly amazing, isn't she?*

For sure, said Jasper. *I wish I knew more about the dragons' spirit world. I have a feeling she isn't really dead, but she's gone to be with your father in another world.*

I hope so, said Bergamen as a single tear slipped down his cheek.

We better get moving again, said Jasper. *My father is going to be plenty mad.*

CHAPTER 3

PURSUIT

Jasper tried to run, but that caused his pack to bounce, which in turn caused Bergamen a lot more pain. Jasper then worked on walking as fast as he could while keeping the pack level and steady, holding it in front of him.

It wasn't long before Jasper felt a stab in his head as his father shouted at him telepathically, *Where are you, you ungrateful wretch?*

Jasper didn't answer, and he did his best to shield himself as Windsong had taught him. Unfortunately, he wasn't strong enough, and soon his father said, *Hah, I will find you. I'm on your trail now. You will pay for this.*

Jasper hurried on as quickly as he could. It was beginning to grow dark, and he knew that he had to find a place to hide them both. The trail was very narrow, and he had to watch out for low branches. It was hard to keep the pack from bouncing, and he couldn't use his arms to steady himself. He was tired and scared. He thought he remembered a cave close by, and he got off the path and worked his way around several boulders, doing his best not to leave a trail. After about thirty minutes, he spied the cave opening. This was not a cave that his father had ever picked for them to stay in, and Jasper hoped it was one he didn't know of.

Jasper pushed several large rocks near the opening of the cave. Then he slipped inside and did his best to position the rocks to disguise the opening. He moved to the very back of the cave and sank down to the floor.

He opened his pack and helped Bergamen out. The poor dragon was obviously in great distress, which caused Jasper pain as well. Jasper gave Bergamen some dried meat, and then he ate an apple for himself. He and Bergamen worked together to try to block Rastan, but it was clear that Rastan was too strong for them. Rastan was getting closer. Jasper had no idea what to do. His father was yelling and shrieking at him, giving him a giant head-ache. *You'll pay for this, boy! I'm nearly to you, and I'll give you a good whipping. I can feel another presence with you. You let that egg hatch, didn't you? Well, I'll get you both, and then I'll kill your little hatchling. How dare you defy me. Your mother tried to defy me, and look where that got her. I didn't need her interfering with how I raised you, but now you're turning out to be just like her. Not only do you look like her, but you're weak and stupid, just as she was when she left.*

Rastan kept taunting him, and Jasper was sure that he did that to keep him listening so he could home in on Jasper's location. Jasper wanted to block his father, but not only was he not strong enough, he also wanted to hear more about his mother. He'd never really known what happened to her. He thought maybe she just couldn't stand the abuse from his father and that she was disappointed in him as well. She'd been so kind and gentle, but he figured that she just got fed up with Rastan.

All of a sudden, his head quieted, and his father was gone. Then both he and Bergamen heard a telepathic voice. *Do you two need help?*

Yes! they answered in unison.

My name is Wilhelmina, and I have now shielded you from Rastan.

You know him? asked Jasper.

Oh, yes, I do, and he's really not a nice person. But let's get you two to safety.

Please, said Bergamen, with just a slight whimper because of the pain.

I've called in the dragons. Sapphire is sending Oscar and Foster out right now. They will distract Rastan and lead him off in another direction. You two just rest and try to get some sleep. I'll keep guard over you.

Thanks, they answered in unison.

Both Bergamen and Jasper were soon sleeping soundly. Wilhelmina, who was a large brown moose with the strongest telepathic magic on the planet, was still several miles away. Nevertheless, she was able to cast a telepathic shield over the cave where Bergamen and Jasper were sleeping so that Rastan lost the trail. As she hoped, when Rastan saw Oscar and Foster flying over him, he assumed that they were going to help his son, so he changed his direction and followed them. This caused him to get farther and farther from Jasper and Bergamen as they slept.

Meanwhile, Wilhelmina contacted Ty to let him know that while she was unclear exactly what was going on, a young lad and a hatchling dragon were in need of assistance. She suggested that he and Criseda meet her at the cave where the travelers were hiding.

As dawn was breaking, Ty and Criseda landed next to Wilhelmina outside the cave where Jasper and Bergamen had taken refuge. Ty went into the cave and gently woke Jasper.

"Who are you?" asked Jasper.

"My name is Ty, and my dragon, Criseda, and I are here to rescue you. Wilhelmina said you needed help."

Bergamen stirred and then looked at Ty, a tall, slim young man with short brown hair and deep brown eyes.

Jasper said, "You have a dragon?"

Ty smiled and said, "Well, she isn't mine, but she and I do work closely together. And you look as if you could use some help. If you come outside, you can meet Criseda and Wilhelmina. They didn't want to try to get through the small cave opening."

"Is it safe?" asked Jasper. "What about my father?"

"Is Rastan your father?" asked Ty.

Jasper nodded.

Ty looked at him and then said, "I'm sorry. However, he won't be able to get to you. You're safe now."

Jasper stood up and gently cradled Bergamen. Ty grabbed Jasper's pack, and the three of them went outside.

Jasper and Bergamen stood staring at both Criseda, who was a large turquoise dragon, and the moose, Wilhelmina. The boy and dragon seemed at a loss as to what to say or do, so Ty took command.

"Jasper, Bergamen, meet Wilhelmina, who shielded you all night so your father couldn't find you, and Criseda, who will fly us to the dragons' aerie, where you, Bergamen, can get some much-needed medical attention and both of you can get some food."

Jasper bowed, and both he and Bergamen thanked Wilhelmina for protecting them.

My pleasure, said Wilhelmina. *I've been keeping an eye on Rastan, and I was really upset that I couldn't stop him from trapping and killing those two dragons, who I suspect were your parents, Bergamen. But we are going to stop him, I promise you.*

Thank you, said Bergamen.

Ty helped Jasper onto Criseda, a task that would have been easier if Jasper had been willing to let Ty hold Bergamen, but Jasper refused. He cradled Bergamen carefully as Criseda bent a front leg and Ty showed Jasper how to climb up the leg and onto Criseda's back.

Then Ty vaulted onto Criseda just in front of Jasper, saying, "Just hold on to my belt with your free hand. We won't let you fall. Wilhelmina, thanks, and will you head back to Dragonwind and let Esme, Martha, and Kyle know to keep an eye out for Rastan? We'll take these two directly to Sapphire."

Sure thing, said Wilhelmina. She turned and headed for the path to Dragonwind.

CHAPTER 4

HEALING

It didn't take long for Criseda to reach the aerie. Flying was certainly faster than walking, and Jasper was very grateful for that, because he was really worried about Bergamen.

Criseda landed in a central flat area that was surrounded by stones. Ty jumped down and then helped Jasper as he said, "I've called for both Sapphire and Blossom. Blossom is the dragons' best healer. Ah, here they come."

Jasper watched as a large blue dragon and a slightly smaller pink dragon approached. He said to Bergamen, *They don't look happy.*

Sapphire looked at them and then turned to Ty. *Thanks, Ty, for rescuing these two. We'll take things from here. Would you please take the boy to Dragonwind? We'll—*

"No!" shouted Jasper. "I'm not leaving."

You'll do as you're told, said Sapphire.

Ty said very quietly, "Sapphire, I don't think that would be a good idea."

What do you mean? asked Sapphire.

"He means..." said Bergamen, and everyone turned to him in shock, as Bergamen was speaking aloud, not telepathically. "He means," continued Bergamen, "that Jasper and I are a pair, and we cannot be separated."

Sapphire was too shocked to answer for a moment, and then she turned to Ty and asked, *What's he talking about? How did this happen?*

Ty said, "I studied them as we flew here, and there's a link between them that's like nothing I've ever seen before. Not only can they communicate telepathically, but it's as if their brains are linked into one larger brain. It's hard to see where one ends and the other begins."

That's impossible, said Sapphire. *No dragon would do that.*

"My mother said we were the first dragon-human pair. She warned us that others would make our life difficult," said Bergamen.

This is Windsong's doing? asked Sapphire.

"No, she just foresaw what we'd become, the first in a new type of relationship. She said others would find it difficult to understand but that it was necessary if our world is going to survive and defeat Rastan."

We'll talk about this later, said Sapphire. *But Jasper must go, at least for now.*

"Then I go with him. We will not be separated," said Bergamen.

Don't be foolish, said Sapphire. *You need medical care.*

Ty stood by the young pair and said, "Martha and I can try to help Bergamen if you insist. But I really think the wisest course is to allow Jasper to remain."

Now you're telling me what to do? snorted Sapphire telepathically.

"Not at all," answered Ty. "I just know that these two can't be separated."

Blossom spoke then. *Sapphire, Ty is correct. Have you ever known a dragon to use human speech?*

Of course not, said Sapphire. *We could, but why should we use such a primitive form of communication? This hatchling just hasn't been properly taught.*

Bergamen turned to Ty and said very firmly, "Can you take us to Dragonwind and the woman you called Martha? I believe we'll find a friendlier home there. Please."

I won't allow you to leave, said Sapphire.

"I don't believe you have any right to hold me. My mother and father left the aerie and were free dragons. So am I, and I have no intention of staying where we aren't wanted."

Ty said, "What's wrong with Jasper staying? Why are you so against it?"

Because this hatchling needs to learn proper dragon protocol, and he can't do that if Jasper stays.

"I respect your boundaries," began Ty, "but the reality is that your efforts to keep dragons out of human affairs have become increasingly difficult, and if I'm honest, you tend to take a superior attitude and wait until situations are desperate before you offer assistance."

We are superior, said Sapphire.

"You sound just like my father," said Jasper, quietly but firmly.

This caused Sapphire to snap her head around and look at Jasper. Then she said, *I'm nothing like Rastan.*

Jasper looked down at the ground under Sapphire's glare, but Bergamen said, "Rastan thinks that he's superior to everyone and everything on this planet. This seems to match your opinion of dragons. He may be evil, and I hope you aren't, but you are both operating from a position of superiority."

Ty chuckled. "He's right, you know."

There's a major difference, said Sapphire. *We are superior and only want what's good for the planet. Rastan is not superior and only wants what's best for him.*

"Maybe that's true," said Bergamen, "but I suspect that the reality is very different. My mother said…"

Your mother was an idealistic fool, said Sapphire.

"Ty, we're leaving now," said Jasper, surprised by his own determination, but he had to help Bergamen. "Can you help us? Obviously this dragon has made up her mind. We do need help. Bergamen needs food, and he's in a lot of pain, and she doesn't seem to care at all."

Ty looked at Sapphire and said, "Well, is Jasper right? If so, I'm taking these two to Martha. I would appreciate it if you'd allow Criseda to transport them, as I think speed is really important, or we'll lose Bergamen."

Get out of here, snapped Sapphire. *Do what you will.*

Criseda bent her leg, and Ty helped Jasper onto her back as Jasper cradled Bergamen. To everyone's surprise, Blossom said, *I'm coming too. I think you and Martha could use my help.*

Sapphire turned her back on them all and stomped away.

"Thanks, Blossom," said Ty, and the two dragons took off and headed to Dragonwind. It was only about ten minutes later that they were landing on the village green in front of Martha's home.

21

Wilhelmina was already there, along with Paul, the seven-year-old boy whom Ty and Wilhelmina had rescued from a mine collapse two years earlier and who now lived in Dragonwind with his mother, Naomi, and others who had been rescued at the same time.

Other villagers came out to see what was going on. Martha rushed over to Ty, along with her ward, Esme, a fifteen-year-old girl who was short and thin, with short brown hair and kind brown eyes and who had special mind-reading magic; and Kyle, a special friend of Martha's who used to live in the woods as a hermit.

Martha, a short, heavyset woman in her midfifties, with gray hair and eyes and a kind, plump face, took charge immediately, asking the villagers to give them all some room and not crowd around. She then asked Ty what Blossom needed and where she wanted to work.

Ty looked at Blossom, who did something quite amazing. She, like Bergamen, began speaking aloud. Martha looked surprised but quickly recovered when Blossom asked if there was an indoor area large enough for her to work.

"Yes," said Martha. "We have several, thanks to Wilhelmina's presence. Paul and Naomi live in a home that easily accommodates Wilhelmina, so it would do for you as well. We also have a village hall, which is very spacious."

"Which is closer?" asked Blossom. "This hatchling needs immediate assistance if we are going to save him."

"This way," said Martha. "The village hall is right next to the tea shop."

Once Martha, Wilhelmina, Blossom, Ty, Esme, Paul, and Kyle got Jasper and Bergamen into the hall, Blossom said, "I'll need a large table, the higher the better."

Kyle, a tall, solidly built man in his midfifties, with hazel eyes, nearly white hair, and a bushy gray beard, said, "Just a moment. I have an idea," and he left the room.

Blossom then said, "I'm going to need some small splints for the wing."

Esme and Paul looked at each other, then ran out of the room.

"I'm going to need a sleeping draft for both Jasper and Bergamen. I know what to use for Bergamen, but would you have something for Jasper?"

"Definitely," said Martha. "Is he also injured?"

"No," said Blossom, "but he will feel every bit of Bergamen's pain. So he needs to be asleep as well."

Blossom asked Ty to mix up the potion she wanted for Bergamen as Martha went to get something for Jasper.

Kyle was the first to return, and he had three other men with him. They were carrying a long counter from the bakery next door. It was taller than a regular table and wider as well. He set it in the middle of the room after clearing other tables and chairs away.

Jasper said, "Blossom, Bergamen is fading in and out of consciousness. He hasn't eaten in several hours."

"Thanks, Jasper," said Blossom. "That situation needs to be remedied first. Kyle—is that your name?"

"Yes, ma'am," answered Kyle.

"Would you be able to get us some warm broth or stew?"

"Certainly." Kyle headed out again, making sure the other men left with him.

Martha returned with a mug of a warm drink to give to Jasper when it was time.

Kyle was back in just a few minutes, and he handed a bowl of warm stew to Jasper, who set it on the table and gently fed Bergamen. At first he had to dribble the liquid into Bergamen's mouth, but soon Bergamen was waking up and demanding more.

Everyone breathed a sigh of relief as the young dragon revived with the food. Blossom checked him over and pronounced that for a dragon who had just hatched the day before, he was in very good shape, except for the broken wing.

"You've done a remarkable job, young Jasper," Blossom said. "I couldn't have done better myself, and neither could his own mother. Can either of you explain how Bergamen's wing was broken?"

Jasper blushed at the compliment. Then he said, "My father kicked the egg away from Windsong, and I caught it just before it went over the cliff.

Esme and Paul came in with a lot of wooden splints. "We got these from Wilson, Dragonwind's carpenter, who had various scraps he thought would work."

Blossom looked at the splints and said, "You did a good job getting these." Then she nodded to Ty and Martha, saying, "OK, time to have these boys take a nap."

"Good luck, Bergamen," said Jasper as he took a mug from Martha.

"Thanks," said Bergamen as Ty helped him gulp down his own tincture.

Soon both Jasper and Bergamen were sleeping on the counter. Blossom then examined the broken wing, with Ty and Martha assisting. Blossom said, "Does anyone know why Rastan kicked Bergamen's egg?

Ty answered, "Jasper said that after Rastan trapped both Windsong and the egg, he chained up Windsong and then just kicked the egg away. I guess Rastan's goal is to eliminate all dragons. Thankfully, Jasper caught the egg just before it fell off the cliff."

"What a beast," said Blossom. "This wing will have to be rebroken. It started to knit together inside the egg, and of course there wasn't room for it to be properly set."

Ty helped her by holding the wing as she directed and then, at her direction, rebroke it. Martha had the splints ready, and between the three of them, they got the wing properly splinted.

"That should do it," said Blossom. "We'll just let the two of them sleep now. You know, truly, I'm amazed that Jasper was able to care for Bergamen so well when they were running from Rastan."

"Jasper told me," said Ty, "that he was too scared to do much until Bergamen encouraged him. I never met Windsong, but she must have been a very remarkable dragon to teach Bergamen so much before he even hatched."

"I always liked Windsong," said Blossom, "and Ventus. I think they were right about how dragons need to change, but as you saw today, that's going to be quite a challenge for us."

"I have to admit that I was surprised by Sapphire's reaction," said Ty.

"I think she'll come around to see that what Bergamen and Jasper have is very special, but I also don't think it will be easy for her to admit that she was wrong, especially now that both Ventus and Windsong are gone."

CHAPTER 5

EARTHQUAKE

Martha made tea and sandwiches for everyone while they waited for Bergamen and Jasper to wake up. It was late afternoon by the time both were awake. Blossom checked Bergamen's splints as he tried to stand and move. He was off balance, but part of that was due to the difference in wing size.

"I'm afraid," said Blossom, "that your left wing will always be smaller. It's not going to grow more to catch up with the right. The two wings, as well as the rest of your body, will all grow at the same rate, so the proportions between your limbs will remain constant."

"Will I be able to fly?" asked Bergamen.

"I'm not sure," said Blossom, giving the young dragon an honest answer. "You may be able to fly, at least short distances, and I guess that if you strengthen your left wing, you may be able to compensate for its smaller size. We'll just have to wait and see how things develop."

Jasper patted Bergamen and said, "I don't care if you can fly or not. As far as I'm concerned, you are the very best dragon in the entire world. I feel so lucky to have you as my partner."

Bergamen tried to smile. Everyone could see that he was disturbed by the smaller wing, but it was Blossom who put things into a better perspective. "I've no idea why your left wing is smaller, but I have seen this condition before. And it has nothing to do with how wonderful a dragon you are, as

Jasper has said. Furthermore, this is not the result of your egg being kicked. You were conceived this way, for whatever reason. Your mother would have known about the smaller wing. Did she ever mention it?"

"No," said Bergamen.

"I can tell you now that it made absolutely no difference to her," said Blossom.

"How can you know that?" asked Bergamen.

"It's simple," said Blossom. "Dragons know exactly what their offspring will be from the moment of conception. She might not have known your color, but she'd know everything else about you. That's how she was able to teach you. Your father would have known as well. And dragons tend to keep any defective dragonets from hatching."

Ty said, "You mean, they kill them?"

Blossom nodded. "It's very sad, but they do it immediately, before the hatchling develops a consciousness. The practice was set up to protect the species and to keep those dragons who truly weren't viable or able to add to the strength of the clan from hatching. The point here is that your parents did not see your smaller wing as an issue. Jasper doesn't see it as an issue. I suspect no one here sees it as a problem. Therefore, you shouldn't worry about it. Once your wing is healed and the bones are strong, I'll be happy to help you develop an exercise regimen so that you get the most benefit from your body."

"Thank you," said Bergamen. "I guess that all makes sense. I feel better knowing that my mom knew. I know she really loved me, so she didn't worry about it either."

"Precisely," said Ty. "I'll tell you now that I was born in an entirely wrong body, so I know a little bit of what you are feeling. I was born into a girl's body, and I hated it. But my parents understood, and they encouraged me to live my life as a boy. After they were killed, when I was six, Martha raised me, and she did the same. Finally, once I brought my parents' murderers to justice, the dragons rewarded me by changing my body into the one that it should have been from the beginning."

"Wow," said Bergamen. "Could the dragons fix my wing?"

"Unfortunately, no," said Blossom. "Dragon physiology is very different. I'm sorry."

Martha said, "I think both of these two need to eat and then rest."

Blossom said, "Definitely. And I'm going to need to return to the aerie. Martha, you can just feed Bergamen as much meat, raw or cooked, as he can eat. He'll need to feed every two to three hours. You can also mix in some greens and vegetables. And please don't hesitate to have Ty contact me if you have any problems or questions. I'm well aware of your healing skills, especially as you tended both Esme and Paul when they were critically ill, so I know Bergamen is in good hands."

Just as Blossom turned to go, there was a tremendous shaking of the ground. Ty shouted, "Earthquake! Get everyone out of here!"

They quickly exited the building and discovered many villagers on the village green. "What's going on?" asked one villager.

"It's an earthquake," said Ty.

Did you feel that, boy? came Rastan's voice inside Jasper's head.

Jasper turned to Ty and Blossom and said, "That was my father's work."

Ty said, "How is that possible?"

"He's a very strong weather mage, and he can cause flooding or droughts, windstorms, blizzards, and yes, even earthquakes," said Jasper.

Blossom said, "I believe this quake was centered at the aerie. I'm getting lots of reports from the other dragons."

"So what we felt is less than what happened up there," said Ty.

Criseda answered, for the first time using human speech, as she said, "I just heard from Sapphire, and the damage at the aerie is significant. Boulders have shifted, caves have collapsed, and there are rockslides. Dragons are trapped inside the collapsed caves, and several have been injured."

"We need to help them," said Martha.

"We also need to find out if any of our villagers have been injured," said Ty.Wilhelmina arrived just then and said, *As far as I can tell, the village has not suffered much damage, and there are no injured humans.*

"OK," said Ty. "I'll fly to the aerie with Criseda and Blossom so we can help. Wilhelmina, will you bring Esme and Paul? I believe their magical skills will help us locate any who might be unconscious."

"I'll come too," said Martha, "once I've made sure that no one here needs my healing skills."

Kyle said, "I believe I should stay here to watch over Jasper and Bergamen. I don't want to discover that this was a ruse on Rastan's part to get Jasper and Bergamen alone."

"Good point," said Ty. "Wilhelmina, stay in touch."

Then Ty vaulted onto Criseda, and they and Blossom took off for the aerie.

Paul and Esme, along with Esme's friends Rupert, a lovely red fox, and Samantha, a beautiful ground squirrel, arrived, reporting that so far the damage was minimal. Things had been knocked off shelves and a few windows cracked, but no one had been injured.

Suddenly Esme stiffened in alarm and said, "There's someone coming for Jasper."

"I knew it," said Kyle.

"It's my father," said Jasper. "He'll never leave me alone."

We'll see about that, said Wilhelmina.

Rastan walked out of the woods and strode to the village green. "Jasper, you'll come with me right now. If you don't, I'll harm your new friends. You wouldn't want that, would you?"

Kyle stepped in front of Jasper and said, "Your son has told us how you've abused him, so no, we won't be turning him over to you."

Esme gasped and then said, "You killed his mother when he was only five! You killed her as soon as Jasper was able to feed and dress himself. You did that because she was trying to protect Jasper from your abuse. You need Jasper because he's got more potential for magic than you do!"

"What?" said Jasper. "He killed my mother! I thought she just left us."

"That's absurd," said Rastan. "I'm a very powerful mage. I don't fear anyone. Jasper, you need to come with me because you know we can't trust anyone else. The world is out to hurt you. These people will turn on you. You need me. And she's telling lies about your mother."

"You may think you're the most powerful mage," said Esme, "but that's only because you've convinced Jasper that he's incompetent and has no talent beyond a little telepathy. You've made sure he's gotten no training, but you're using his power to add to yours."

Rastan looked stunned and finally said, "How can you say that?"

"Because I can read your evil mind. Anyone who would kill a small child's mother to further his own ends is the lowest life form there is," said Esme. "Jasper, I'm sorry. I didn't know that you didn't know your mother had been killed by your father."

"Are you sure?" said Jasper.

Esme nodded.

Then Bergamen said, "I'm sorry, Jasper, but she's right. My mother told me, but I haven't had a chance to let you know."

Kyle put a comforting arm on Jasper's shoulder as Wilhelmina moved to stand with Jasper, Bergamen, Esme, Martha, and Kyle and said, *You are also not the strongest telepath on the planet. I've been tracking you for years, trying to keep Jasper safe. You aren't even as strong as the dragons. Your telepathic range is mediocre at best.*

"I'm not mediocre at anything," said Rastan. "You will all regret this. The earthquake I caused is just the beginning. I will wreak such havoc that you will all starve to death. Then we'll see who has the power."

"What good will it do you to have power over a dead planet?" said Kyle in a reasonable tone.

"What do you care? You won't be around," said Rastan.

Jasper tried to say something, but Bergamen spoke to him telepathically. *Don't talk to him. He's trying to scare you. He wants you to give in to save your friends, but don't. You are not responsible for his actions, and your friends are doing their best to protect you.*

But if I go, you will all be safe, said Jasper.

No, we won't, said Wilhelmina. *He's going to try to kill us all with or without you.*

Esme said, *Wilhelmina is correct. I can read his intentions, and he only wants you because he's afraid of you and your power.*

My power? I don't have any power, said Jasper.

That's what he wants you to believe, said Esme. *That's why he killed your mother. She would have taught you about magic. Now just let Kyle and Wilhelmina work this out.*

Rastan tried another argument. "Jasper is my son. You have no right to keep him from me. You can keep that runt of a deformed dragon, but my son is coming with me."

"We have every right," said Martha. "I've already had to deal with abusive parents when I became Esme's guardian. King Bertram has no tolerance for unfeeling parents trying to take advantage of their child's talents. I'm giving my protection to Jasper until I can contact King Bertram and apprise him of the situation."

"Now get out of here," said Kyle.

Rastan laughed. Then he threw a fireball at the group. Without even thinking, Jasper summoned a nearby rain barrel and poured water over the fireball. It was hard to say who looked more shocked, Rastan or Jasper.

"You!" said Rastan. "What did you do?"

"Protected my friends," said Jasper in a voice that quavered only a bit. Then he continued. "I will not go with you. You are an evil murderer, and I'm ashamed that you are my father."

Rastan sneered, "You'll be sorry." He turned to leave, and as he did so, he closed his eyes and frowned in concentration, and again the ground shook, but this time the earthquake was centered right in the village. Several buildings collapsed, including Martha's cottage two doors down from the village hall. Screams could be heard from a number of spots, but the only thing those on the village green registered was Rastan's maniacal laughter as he walked away.

Kyle and Martha raced to the screams. Others came to help as well. Esme and Paul sent out telepathic searches for anyone trapped under debris. This time the village wasn't so lucky. In addition to Martha's cottage, there were a number of other collapsed buildings. There were also lots of broken windows. Thankfully the only injuries were minor. People had been outside for the most part, trying to see if their buildings had any damage from the first earthquake.

Wilhelmina kept Jasper and Bergamen close beside her and then contacted Ty. *There's been a change of plan. Rastan showed up here and tried to get Jasper. Turns out that Jasper has a lot of latent magical talent, and Rastan has been verbally and physically abusing him to keep him from finding out how gifted he is. Anyway, Rastan*

30

caused another earthquake, which you must have felt, but this time the village was its center, and there is a lot of damage. Thankfully the injuries are minor, but I think we need to stay here. I don't think it's a good idea to leave Jasper and Bergamen unguarded.

I agree, said Ty. *Things here aren't so bad. A couple of dragons are trapped in their caves, but they aren't injured, and the other dragons are freeing them. A few did suffer injuries, but they were really minor, and Blossom has tended to them. Sapphire isn't at all happy with the latest developments, so it's best if Jasper and Bergamen stay in Dragonwind. I'll be down as soon as I can. Not sure if Criseda will come with me or stay here.*

I understand, said Wilhelmina.

Wilhelmina then turned to Jasper and Bergamen. *I bet the two of you are hungry. It looks as if the tea shop and bakery are still standing. Let's see if there's anyone to help us find food.*

"Is all this my fault?" asked Jasper.

"No!" shouted Bergamen.

Definitely not, agreed Wilhelmina.

CHAPTER 6

KIDNAP

The villagers were all on edge as the earthquakes continued over the next few days. The quakes were smaller but no less unnerving. Thankfully there was no major damage or injuries.

Wilson, as the lead carpenter in Dragonwind, was overseeing the repairs to the buildings that had been damaged. The entire village came together to work on a new home for Martha. Hers was the only cottage to be totally destroyed, and all the villagers knew what a debt they owed her. Not only had she delivered many of the villagers, she'd also treated all of them at one time or another.

Ty was even more on edge than the others because he was unable to contact Criseda. He went in search of Wilhelmina, and when he found her on the village green, he asked her, "Do you know what's happening with the dragons?"

No, she answered. *I've tried to make contact with Sapphire, but she's blocking me completely. I don't like the way she's isolating them.*

Just then Blossom landed beside them. "I've come to see Bergamen and be sure he's healing properly. I also wanted to update you on what's going on in the aerie."

"I can't contact Criseda," said Ty, panic evident in his voice.

"I know," said Blossom. "Sapphire has closed down the aerie, forbidding any contact, either in person or telepathically, with humans."

"What?" said Ty.

I was afraid of that, said Wilhelmina.

"She's panicking," said Blossom. "The changes Bergamen and Jasper demonstrated are just too much for her to handle. The earthquakes aren't helping, and Rastan's threats have her very worried."

"Doesn't she realize that we need to work together to figure this out?" asked Ty.

"Sapphire has always ruled with her iron will, but now she's terrified that she'll lose control of the dragons. The fact that Windsong and Ventus were able to survive on their own, at least until running into Rastan, is proof that dragons don't have to live in the aerie. Then Windsong's teaching of Bergamen and her knowing about the ability of dragons and humans to link themselves has shaken her deeply," said Blossom.

"What can we do?" asked Ty. "I have to see Criseda."

"I agree," said Blossom. "Criseda needs you. She's refusing to eat, and she's getting weak. I'm very concerned. You and Criseda have a different kind of bond from what Jasper and Bergamen have. It isn't quite as strong, and yours grew slowly rather than the instant bond they have, but neither you nor Criseda can do well without the other."

Ty is barely eating, and then only enough to keep Martha from force-feeding him, said Wilhelmina.

"How did you manage to leave the aerie if Sapphire has it locked down?" asked Ty.

"She wouldn't dare interfere with me. I'm one of the oldest dragons, and I remember when she was a hatchling. Furthermore, I don't need to stay in the aerie. I'm not afraid to go out on my own, as Windsong did. Sapphire needs me a lot more than I need her, since I'm the best healer," said Blossom. "Now let's go see Bergamen and Jasper. Where are they?"

"They're in the town hall for the moment," said Ty. "We set up a temporary residence for Martha in one corner of the big room."

The three of them walked over to the town hall and entered as Martha was handing a bowl of stew to Jasper so he could help Bergamen eat.

"Hi, Blossom," said Bergamen cheerfully. "Martha is the best cook."

Blossom chuckled and said, "Well, her food certainly seems to agree with you. I think you're about twice the size you were when I saw you two days ago."

Bergamen puffed out his chest and said, "I'm going to be really big soon."

Jasper rubbed the top of Bergamen's head and said, "You sure will be."

"It looks as if the two of you are doing just fine," said Blossom. "Does your wing hurt, Bergamen?"

"Not really," he said. "As long as I don't bump it or swing it around. The splints help a lot, although they do make me a bit clumsy."

"That's understandable," said Blossom. "Keep on eating, and I'll be back to see you in a few days."

Wilhelmina, Ty, and Blossom went outside. Blossom said, "I'll be happy to carry messages between you and Criseda until this is sorted out."

"Thanks," said Ty. "Please tell her to eat and look after herself. I couldn't bear it if anything happened to her. Sapphire has got to see reason soon."

"I hope so," said Blossom. "I'll be sure to tell Criseda that you miss her and are worried about her, as I'm sure she is about you. I'd better get back now. The dragons are very restless, because Sapphire won't let them leave the aerie, and most of them are used to flying every day."

The situation does seem to be potentially explosive, said Wilhelmina. *If you can think of any way we can help, please let us know.*

"And look after Criseda for me," pleaded Ty.

▲

Sapphire was worried. She didn't trust humans, although she had to admit that there were good people in Dragonwind. Nevertheless, she felt she needed to keep the dragons separate. She couldn't understand this new bond between Bergamen and Jasper. She didn't really like how close Criseda had gotten to Ty. It just wasn't natural, and she needed to keep dragons safe and as far from humans as possible. She wasn't sure what she should do, but she knew she had to get Bergamen before he was totally corrupted by humans. She left the aerie in the middle of the night, flew directly to Dragonwind, and quietly entered the town hall. She quickly moved over to Bergamen, bundled him into a blanket, ignored the screams from Jasper as she left the building, and flew back to the aerie.

You'll stay with us now, and I'll have none of your cheek or your human speech. Do you understand?

"No, and I won't do anything for you."

Sapphire tied a rope around Bergamen's left leg and then staked the rope to the ground inside her own cave.

Bergamen tried to call for Jasper telepathically, but Sapphire blocked him. *Don't think anyone will hear you. I will block communications with any humans.*

Sapphire then left her cave to keep watch over the aerie, lest any of her dragons try to leave. She had to keep them here, safe from the likes of Rastan, for their own good. They might not like it, but she did know what she was doing, and it was what they needed.

▲

Jasper started screaming as soon as Sapphire touched Bergamen. Unfortunately, it took several minutes to get help. Martha ran for Ty and Wilhelmina, but by then Sapphire was well away.

Jasper was in tears. "I can't reach him!" he said. "I need to find him."

Ty said, "I think we all know where he's gone. Sapphire will be blocking all communications in and out of the aerie, so we'll have to find another way to reach him."

"He's so little," said Jasper. "He needs me."

Martha put an arm around Jasper and said, "We know that he needs you, and you need him. Ty and Wilhelmina will find him and bring him back. Now, you need to get back into bed. Things will look better in the morning."

"But..." protested Jasper, but Martha turned him back to his bed and tucked him in.

"Ty and Wilhelmina will find him. You need to trust them," said Martha.

Ty called to him, "We will get him, Jasper!"

With that, Ty and Wilhelmina left the hall, and Martha went back to bed after making sure that Jasper was going to sleep.

Jasper pretended to be asleep until he heard Martha's deep breathing. Then he grabbed his coat, slipped on his boots, and left the hall. He took the path out of the village and began to climb it toward the aerie. He couldn't leave Bergamen alone. He couldn't trust anyone to find Bergamen.

It was dark and Jasper stumbled a lot, but he kept going. In places the path was narrow, and there was a sharp drop-off in many spots, so he had to be very careful. He'd been hiking for about an hour, he guessed, when he heard a voice in his head. *Well, son, nice of you to come to me.*

Jasper gasped and turned to run, but he had no idea where his father was or which direction he should run in. Instead he shouted telepathically, as loudly as he could, *Help!*

He only managed to get one shout out before his father struck him, knocking him unconscious.

▲

Esme sat up in bed and hugged Rupert, the red fox who lived with her and Samantha, a gray squirrel, and then she called out telepathically, *Ty, Jasper has left Dragonwind. He's trying to get to the aerie, but he was just knocked unconscious by his father.*

Thanks, Esme. I should have predicted that Jasper wouldn't wait for us to rescue Bergamen. Can you ask Rupert and Samantha to try to track Rastan? Wilhelmina and I are heading to the aerie for Bergamen.

Right away.

Esme turned to Rupert and Samantha and said, *You need to activate the fox-squirrel network and find Rastan and Jasper. Be careful. Rastan plans to force Jasper to help him. He's realized, if I read his mind correctly, that Jasper has stronger magic than he does, so he's going to force Jasper to do his bidding before he realizes his own potential.*

You can count on us, said Rupert, and the two of them headed out for the aerie to pick up Jasper's trail.

Esme tried to go back to sleep, but she was too worried about both Jasper and Bergamen. She put her efforts into trying to contact one or the other of them. She first tried Jasper, but he was still unconscious.

She then tried Bergamen, only to run into the telepathic wall that Sapphire had set up. But Esme was determined. Next she tried to reach Blossom. She found another telepathic wall, but it wasn't as specific or as tough to break through. It was apparently the communication wall Sapphire had set up for all the dragons.

Once she made a dent in the second wall, she sent out a call to Blossom. *Blossom, I need to speak with you. This is Esme.*

How did you managed to reach me? asked Blossom.

Sapphire doesn't have as strong a block on the aerie as she thinks. She also isn't as strong a telepath as I am, since I can not only do telepathy but also read minds. But that's not the point. Sapphire has kidnapped Bergamen.

What!

And it gets worse. Jasper went after Bergamen to try to rescue him, but Rastan found him, knocked him unconscious, and has now taken him somewhere else, and we aren't sure where, although Rupert and Samantha are getting the foxes and squirrels to look for him.

My goodness, said Blossom.

Ty and Wilhelmina are heading your way, but it will take them nearly an hour to get there, since they don't have any way to fly. Can you help? Bergamen must be terrified.

Blossom sighed and then said, *I'll go speak to Sapphire right now. This has gone on long enough. She's a fool, and I think I'm about the only one who can talk sense into her. At least I hope I can. I'll let you know what I find out.*

Thanks, Blossom, and good luck.

▲

Blossom hurried out of her cave and headed for Sapphire's. When she entered Sapphire's cave, she discovered a sobbing Bergamen tied to a stake but no Sapphire. She quickly untied Bergamen and tried to comfort him, but all he would say was, "Rastan has Jasper. He knocked him unconscious, and I can't reach him!"

"I know, sweetie," said Blossom. "Lots of folks, including Rupert, Samantha, Wilhelmina, and Ty, are helping. Now let's get you out of here, and I'll take you to my cave until morning."

Blossom carefully cradled the small dragon in her right front claw and headed for the door. Sapphire walked in and said, *What do you think you're doing?*

Trying to save you from yourself. Can't you see how much you are hurting the community you say you care about?

I'm trying to save our community!

You're fracturing it. You are trying to imprison us within the world as you see it. You know, Bergamen was correct in one way when he said you were just like Rastan. You think you are superior to all others, and you're afraid of losing that power. You don't realize that until this moment we all respected your leadership. But now you're turning into a tyrant. You are clinging to the past, and it's time to move on. I know you were hurt when Windsong and Ventus left. But they saw what was coming. Our world needs to work together, all of us, all species.

But how can we?

We can learn. And this young dragon can help us if you're willing to open yourself to change.

Sapphire snarled in frustration. *Why do things have to change?*

That's rather the nature of life, said Blossom wryly.

"What about Jasper?" shouted Bergamen.

What about him? snapped Sapphire. *I didn't take him.*

"No, but you're why he's now unconscious and kidnapped by his father!" said Bergamen. "Are you going to help find him?"

Sapphire looked over at Blossom, tilting her head in puzzlement.

Blossom said, "When you kidnapped Bergamen, Jasper called for help. Ty, Martha, and Wilhelmina came right away, but, according to Esme, who by the way was able to avoid your telepathic wards to talk with me—"

What? said Sapphire in shock.

"Yes, that's what I'm trying to tell you. The world is changing, and there are others who can do what you do, or at least some of it. Anyway, Martha put Jasper back to bed, telling him to let Ty and Wilhelmina handle things. However, the young never really listen, and Jasper was really hurting without Bergamen and scared that you'd do something horrible, so he headed out on his own to confront you. His father caught him on the path and knocked him unconscious. So now Rupert, a fox, and Samantha, a squirrel, are tracking Rastan and Jasper while Ty and Wilhelmina try to break in here and save Bergamen, as well as Criseda, who is getting weaker and weaker without access to Ty. Ty and Criseda have developed a strong empathic bond. Neither is truly whole without the other. It's different from what Bergamen and Jasper have, but the reality is that neither can thrive and maybe not even live without the other."

Sapphire plopped down on the ground, stunned. Finally she said, *I did all this just by capturing Bergamen so I could teach him to be a proper dragon?*

"Proper by whose standards?" said Bergamen. "I'm a perfectly proper dragon. My mother said so."

"I think that this discussion needs to wait. What we need now is to let Ty and Wilhelmina know that Bergamen is safe, that you're taking down your blocking spells, and that Criseda can join Ty so that they and Wilhelmina can follow Rupert and Samantha to rescue Jasper. Nothing else matters at the moment," said Blossom.

I only tried to keep the dragons safe, said Sapphire. *Humans can be vengeful and violent. I didn't want the dragons to get dragged into their world. Dragons have suffered at the hands of humans in the past. I thought I could raise Bergamen here. I had no idea that all this would happen. I've been a fool. Can you forgive me?*

Definitely, Blossom said telepathically to reinforce her concern for Sapphire. "Now let's get going."

CHAPTER 7

RESCUE

Sapphire immediately contacted Ty. *Ty, Bergamen is safe with us. Blossom has him. I'm send-ing Criseda to you. Apparently, Rupert and Samantha are trying to track Rastan and Jasper. Please find Jasper, and then bring him here.*

Sapphire? Is that really you?

Yes. I admit I've been a fool, but the important thing now is to rescue Jasper. We'll talk later.

Thanks, Sapphire.

Then Sapphire, Blossom, and Bergamen went to Criseda's cave. Sapphire saw immediately that Blossom was correct. Criseda was failing. She woke as they entered.

Sapphire went right over to Criseda and said, *I've failed you. I've failed our community. But right now I need you, if you're able, to fly to Ty and Wilhelmina, who are on the path to our aerie, and help them rescue Jasper, who's been kidnapped by his father.*

Criseda stood. She wobbled a bit but nodded. *Right away, and thanks.*

Blossom said, *You won't go very far if you don't eat something first. It will only take a few minutes. I left you some dried meat earlier tonight.*

Criseda nodded, downed the meat, and headed for the courtyard.

Bergamen said, "Please find Jasper! I need him, and he needs me!"

▲

41

Criseda landed by Wilhelmina and Ty. Wilhelmina said, *It sure is good to see you again!*

Ty ran up to her and reached up to rub her back. Then he said, "We have to find Jasper."

Wilhelmina said, *I'll head back to Dragonwind and let Martha and Esme know that you two are together again.*

"Thanks," said Ty, and then he and Criseda took flight. As they flew, Ty contacted Rupert. *Do you know where Rastan and Jasper are?*

Yes, we found his cave easily enough, and it's not far away. But he has Jasper chained up in the very back of the cave, so it will be hard to get him out without fighting Rastan, which doesn't seem like a good idea right now.

We'll be right with you. Just wait for us.

Rupert was right, and it didn't take Criseda long to land near the cave. Ty jumped down and went over to Rupert.

Have you found out anything more? asked Ty.

Not really, answered Rupert. *We've been listening, and all we've heard is Rastan yelling at Jasper, telling him what a failure he is and how he's never going to be free again.*

Poor Jasper, said Ty.

Just then they heard a large crash from inside the cave, followed by a scream from Rastan. *"How did you get free?"*

▲

Jasper stared in amazement at his hands, turning them this way and that. "I just pulled on the chains, and they came out of the wall," he said, sounding just as surprised as Rastan was.

"You can't do that," said Rastan. "You don't have any *real* magical talents."

"Well, maybe I do," said Jasper. And with that Jasper lifted an arm and waved it toward his father. The result was astonishing. Rastan flew across the cave and crashed into a side wall.

Then Jasper heard Bergamen speak to him telepathically from Blossom's cave. *Be careful, Jasper. My mom told me about your powers and how they would activate now that you're nearly grown. She also warned me to guard you so that you don't become like your father.*

I'll never be like him, said Jasper. *I'm just going to teach him a lesson.*

No, said Bergamen. *If you do, then you will become the bully. This happens some-times to those who have been abused, and you have been very badly treated. But you are a good person. You need to learn about your magic now and use it for good.*

But he's evil, insisted Jasper. *He deserves punishment.*

He certainly does, but not this way. You're reacting with vengeance and not justice. Please! Ty and Criseda are outside. Get out of that cave, and let them bring you here. Lots has been happening, and I want you with me. Please!

Ty could hear all that Bergamen said, and he suspected that Bergamen had meant him to. But he waited quietly outside. This had to be Jasper's decision.

My mom said that the awakening of your powers would be a turning point for you. She said that it would be the most dangerous moment for you, for your soul. Please, Jasper, come back to me.

Jasper looked at his father, who was now trying to stand up. He thought about how his life was changing and how much he wanted to be back with Bergamen. Finally, he started walking toward the cave entrance. As he got closer to his father, he was gratified to see his father back up a bit, but Jasper didn't do anything. He just walked past and out into the forest.

He saw Ty and Criseda, with Rupert and Samantha, and he went over to them. Ty gave him a big hug and said, "Well done."

Ty helped Jasper onto Criseda and then vaulted up in front of him. Rastan came out of his cave and said, "Don't think I'm going to stop. I will get my family's lands back, and nothing will get in my way—not even you, even if I have to kill you all!"

"Try away," said Ty, and Criseda took off as Rupert and Samantha ran down the path to Dragonwind.

Once they were in the air, Ty asked Jasper, "So, how are you doing?"

"I don't know," said Jasper. "I can't believe that I broke those chains. I know they were small chains. He's used them before. But I've never been able to get out of them. What's happening to me?"

"I suspect," said Ty, "that as you're reaching physical maturity, your latent magical powers are finally surfacing. I think that the stress you've been under, as well as your father's actions, have accelerated the development of your powers. The times you've been able to use them have been times when you were threatened."

"I guess that makes sense," said Jasper. "I've never been able to stand up to my father before. I can barely talk to him."

"That's understandable," said Ty. "He's an abuser and a bully."

"I really wanted to kill him," said Jasper. "And I think I would have if Bergamen hadn't stepped in."

"Your dragon knows you well," said Ty. "He knows that you are a gentle soul who abhors violence. If you'd hurt your father, it would have changed you, and not for the better."

Criseda landed in the aerie, and Ty was glad to see that Blossom was there with Bergamen. He helped Jasper get down, and Jasper ran over to Bergamen, saying, "Thank you so much. Are you OK?"

"I am now," said Bergamen. "I was really scared and upset, but then Blossom found me and talked with Sapphire, and everything is good, at least now that you're back."

Sapphire walked over to the pair and said, *I really need to apologize to the four of you, Criseda, Ty, Jasper, and Bergamen. Bergamen was right. I was acting just like Rastan, even if I was doing it for different reasons. I was afraid of the changes I was seeing. I wanted to keep everything the same. In the process of trying to do that, I hurt those I care about.*

"We understand," said Ty, "and it takes a great leader to admit mistakes." Then his face shifted from reassuring to businesslike. "Now we need to discuss how we're going to stop Rastan."

As he said that, another earthquake shook the aerie.

"I agree," said Criseda. "I'm getting really tired of these earthquakes."

"My father can do much worse," said Jasper. "Thankfully, he's so far not been able to make a really big earthquake. His attempts are usually like this, more tremors than strong quakes."

Blossom said, "So, should I ask, what else can he do?"

"He can really mess with the weather. He can make snowstorms, at least in the winter. He can do tons of rain, primarily in the spring. And he can bring droughts that last all summer long and even into the fall."

Sapphire looked at the group, and then, hesitantly, she spoke aloud for the first time. "So how can we stop him? I could stop him if I could make eye contact with him, but unless I can see him, I can't stop him."

"He did show up in Dragonwind briefly after the first earthquake, but unless we can find him, we have a problem. He never stays anywhere for more than a few days, and he keeps moving. I think he does that so that he can't be captured. I don't think you can stop him until we capture him," said Jasper miserably.

"There has to be a way," said Criseda.

Blossom said, "I think this is what Windsong was telling us. I remember just before she left to follow Ventus, she told me that she foresaw major changes in our world, changes that we weren't prepared to handle. She told me that we would need other kinds of magic and that we would even need the talents of those without magic. I think I'm beginning to see what she meant."

Ty looked over at Bergamen and Jasper before saying, "And I think we need to get these two trained as quickly as we can. I have some ideas about that."

Sapphire nodded at him and said, "Let's hear your ideas."

"Well," Ty began, "Bergamen obviously needs to get bigger, but I see that he's doing his best with that."

Blossom chuckled and said, "He's eating us out of house and home for sure."

Ty said, "And we need him to remember everything his mother taught him before he hatched. We don't have another being who's got the ability to see into the future, unfortunately. Windsong was the only source we had."

"That's true," said Sapphire, "and I always doubted the truth of her message, I'm sorry to say."

"And we need to train Jasper to use his magic whenever he needs to and not just when he's under threat. I'm not sure what kinds of magic he'll develop, but we know he has the gifts of telepathy and telekinesis, at the very least. I'd like to see him work with both Wilhelmina and Esme, who comes about the closest we have to foreknowledge in her ability to sense the intentions of others."

"It would be easier for Wilhelmina to work with Jasper in Dragonwind. The mountain path to get here is steep and arduous, and while I know she has done it and can do it again, I also know that Paul needs her," said Sapphire.

"Bergamen still needs to learn about being a dragon," said Blossom.

Sapphire said, "Very true."

"You aren't going to try to split us up again, are you?" said Bergamen.

Sapphire laughed and said, "No, I've learned my lesson. I think we'll need to have Blossom and Criseda work with you in Dragonwind."

Suddenly Jasper stiffened. *You think you've gotten away from me,* came his father's telepathic voice. *You will never get free of me. I'll haunt every moment of your life. And I know you disobeyed me and rescued that dragon egg. I saw what you have, and he's is a very poor excuse for a dragon. He's a runt with a damaged, deformed wing. He'll be my next kill.*

Jasper looked at Ty in a panic. Ty put an arm on his shoulder and said, "Don't worry, we heard him. I'm sure he meant for us all to hear him. We will make sure Bergamen is kept safe until he's grown enough to protect himself."

Sapphire looked at the small dragon in Jasper's hands and said, "Bergamen, I want you to know that everything Rastan said about you is wrong. You are not a poor excuse for a dragon, and the more I learn about you, the prouder I am to know you. I'm sure Blossom has told you that dragons tend to be sure that those dragons who can't survive never hatch. Your mother knew from the beginning just what you would grow up to be, and she was proud of that. She taught you a lot more than we normally do to dragons before they hatch, because her foresight let her know that she wouldn't be here to teach you later. She wouldn't have done that if she hadn't known from the start what an exceptional dragon you will grow up to be."

Blossom smiled and said, "I totally agree, and may I say, I'm also very glad that we have Sapphire leading us."

"Thanks," said Sapphire. "Sorry I went off the rails for a bit, and thanks for getting me back on track. Now, I think these two young ones need to get to Dragonwind. It's been a difficult night for them."

Ty nodded and put Jasper and Bergamen on Criseda's back, then vaulted up in front of them, and Criseda took off.

CHAPTER 8

SNOWSTORM

It was still dark as Criseda landed on the village green. Ty helped Jasper and Bergamen down and then took them into the town hall to the area that had been set up for Martha.

Martha ran over to them and said, "I'm so glad you are safe. I bet you're both hungry, and I have some hot stew waiting for you, since Ty alerted me to your arrival. Well, actually, to be totally honest, he called to Wilhelmina, who then told Paul, who then came over to tell me, but it amounts to the same thing, doesn't it?"

Jasper could see that Martha was flustered and also worried about their safety, so he just said, "Yes, it does, and yes, we are starving, and your food is the best!"

Ty went outside to talk with Criseda and Wilhelmina, and they were also joined by Kyle. Ty said, "We're going to have to guard those two closely, just the way we had to do with Esme when The Wraith was after her. I'll see if Jeb would be willing to help, and I'm sure Rupert and Samantha will alert their friends in the area."

Kyle shook his head and said, "It never seems to end, does it? We get rid of The Wraith, and now we have an evil mage."

"And this mage," said Criseda, watching Kyle start as he heard her voice for the first time, "is going to be changing our weather. He's a weather mage, and his actions could really destroy things. He can not only do the earthquakes we're all getting very tired of, but apparently he can cause various storms, floods, droughts, and heaven knows what else."

"That's not good," said Kyle.

"No, it's not," agreed Ty. "The only good thing about it is that apparently he can only modify the weather. So, for instance, he can't make it snow in the summer. Since we're now into winter, I suspect we'll see lots of snow, sleet, ice, and strong winds. We need to prepare Dragonwind for a very severe winter."

"I'll talk with Wilson and his group of carpenters to see what we can do," said Kyle. "They are nearly finished with Martha's new cottage. She's hoping to move into it in the next day or so. There are still a number of damaged buildings and homes from these blasted earthquakes, but we can also get to winterizing everything. All the villagers will pitch in to help, I'm sure."

"Let's call a village meeting for tomorrow evening, and we can start planning then," said Ty.

▲

The next evening the villagers gathered in the town hall to hear Ty explain what they would be facing. Once he'd finished his presentation, he took questions. It was soon clear that many of the villagers really didn't believe that anyone could control the weather.

"This just isn't possible," said one villager.

"No one has that much power," said another.

"I don't even think this so-called mage is making the earthquakes," said a third. "We get earthquakes fairly commonly anyway. True, we don't usually get this many, but it's not unheard of, especially if there's a mine collapse, which there may very well have been."

Ty held up a hand for silence. "I know this seems impossible, but we do need to be prepared just in case. We will all be better off if we make sure everything is winterized. That's just a sensible precaution, which we should do each and every year. Why don't we start there, and then see what happens? Is that a reasonable plan?"

Those who didn't believe in Rastan's power nevertheless saw the wisdom of getting ready for winter, so a plan was put in place.

Wilhelmina said, *I can't believe that they don't take this threat seriously. We've never had this many earthquakes before, and not this frequently. We're getting nearly one a day, which is way beyond anything we've ever had.*

"I know," said Ty. "It seems that some people will just bury their heads in the sand, so to speak, and do anything to avoid something unpleasant. They will discover all too soon that the weather is going to cause great problems unless we can stay on top of it."

Ty's statement was proven true much sooner than he would have thought possible. Late that night strong winds started howling around the village, and by morning there was about a foot of snow, with lots more falling throughout the next day. Dragonwind was caught in a blizzard.

Wilhelmina used her size to push through some of the drifts between houses. Jeb, the forest steward, moved into town from his cabin in the woods. The forest could take care of itself, and he knew that another hand on a shovel would be welcome. He would stay at Martha's, where he could help guard Jasper and Bergamen.

Ty also stayed in town, since it would be very hard to get to his cave on the outskirts of Dragonwind. He and Criseda did fly to his cave long enough to grab some clothes and, more importantly, to get his black cat, Foxy. She was not happy with all the snow.

I thought you forgot me, said Foxy.

Ty picked her up off his bed and hugged her, saying, "I could never forget you. Would you like to stay at Martha's with Esme, Rupert, and Samantha? Jeb and I will be there as well."

Definitely, she answered. *Martha's cottage is going to be filled.*

"Yes, it will be, but thankfully her new cottage has three bedrooms, not two like her old one, so Martha and Kyle will have their room, you'll be bunking with Esme, Rupert, and Samantha, and then Jeb and I will have part of the third bedroom, with Jasper and Bergamen in the other part."

Is her new cottage finished?

"Basically, yes. She moved in when we saw the snow this morning. There's still some interior finishing details to be done, but we can live with that. Now let's get out of here. Criseda is going to have a hard enough time flying in this blizzard."

As they were flying, Foxy asked, *Where's Criseda going to stay?*

"Naomi and Paul have asked her to stay with them and Wilhelmina. There will be room for both Wilhelmina and Criseda."

That's good, said Foxy as she burrowed into Ty's jacket.

▲

The storm lasted for four days. This did a lot to convince the doubters of Rastan's power.

"We've never had a storm this bad," they said.

Ty wasn't happy about the storm, but he was at least glad that the village was all pulling together and had been convinced of the emergency. Criseda did manage to work with both Bergamen and Jasper, helping them to learn about the planet, its history with the dragons, and a bit of geography, letting them know that they were now in Dragonwind, which was a part of the country of Estrea.

Blossom didn't try to leave the aerie. The dragons were safe, but there was even more snow in the aerie than there was in Dragonwind, so the dragons just stayed in their caves, trying to keep the openings unblocked.

Finally, when the storm ended, both the aerie and Dragonwind had a lot of digging out to do. Jasper was trying to help clear the path from Martha's front door when his father broke in. *Having fun? Is your runty dragon making you do all the work? Do your friends realize that all this snow is your fault? You should never have run away.*

This time Rastan made sure that Jasper was the only one who heard him. He'd realized that his son would be hurt more if his friends didn't hear the taunts. He'd be all alone with no support when Rastan attacked him.

Jasper didn't answer his father. He just kept shoveling. However, Wilhelmina was constantly tuned to any telepathic communications, especially from Rastan, and she heard him taunting Jasper. She didn't let Rastan know that his shield didn't stop her from listening in. Instead she walked over to Martha's and said, *Want some help, Jasper? You're doing a great job, but that's a lot of snow.*

Then Wilhelmina looked right at Jasper and said, *I've blocked out your father. He doesn't know that I heard him. He's so full of himself and thinks he's smarter than any of us, but he hasn't a clue. We're here for you and Bergamen, Jasper. You are both loved.*

Jasper smiled and nodded, and then the two of them worked on the path from Martha's door. While they were working, Wilhelmina contacted Ty. *We need to be sure that Jasper is never left alone. Rastan just blasted another abusive telepathic message at him. I know eventually Jasper will be able to block Rastan out and also not let Rastan's words bother him, but right now he's very fragile.*

I agree, answered Ty. *I think it would be great if Esme befriended him. They seem to be getting along well at Martha's. I'll explain some of this to Esme and see what she thinks.*

Thanks, Ty.

Ty immediately located Esme and updated her on what was happening with Rastan.

"That man is evil," said Esme. "Jasper and Bergamen are so wonderful. Why would anyone want to hurt them?"

"Actually, as you've already discovered, Rastan is afraid of Jasper, afraid that Jasper has more magical power than he does. So he's beating Jasper down so Jasper doesn't realize his own potential. You went through something similar, so do you think you might be able to help Jasper? Just being his friend and helping him see how strong he really is would be great."

"I'd be happy to try," said Esme. "I'm not sure that I can tell when Rastan yells telepathically at Jasper, but I bet Wilhelmina can, and she can always then let me know if she's not able to get to him. We'll protect him and Bergamen."

"You are the best, Esme! Thanks."

CHAPTER 9

WINTER

It was proving to be a very long winter, thanks to Rastan. Ty projected that at the rate the storms were hitting, by the end of winter the village would have nine times more snow than Dragonwind's average of fifty-six inches. However, Ty, Criseda, Wilhelmina, Blossom, and Sapphire were not idle. They met one sunny morning several weeks after the storms had begun for a planning session about how to deal with Rastan. It was a rare moment with no snowstorm. Sapphire started things out by wondering why there seemed to have been an increase in the amount of magic in the world.

"Do you think there really is more magic, or are we just noticing it more?" she asked.

Wilhelmina said, *I believe the amount of magic is growing, and it's also changing. We have not only dragon magic, which I guess we've always had since the dragons started helping humans, but now we have many more animals who are telepathic. We also are discovering more humans with magic of yet another kind. Ty was nearly unique, with his healing magic and telepathy. King Bertram, maybe because of his fairy ancestors, has a very weak telepathic ability as well.*

"However," said Ty, "his abilities are growing, as are Paul's. You were able to reach Paul telepathically just from the strength of your own magic, Wilhelmina. However, since he's been living in Dragonwind, his abilities have really grown. He can now speak telepathically to all of us, although his range is still limited. I expect, though, that his abilities will continue to expand."

"And what about Esme?" asked Sapphire. "Her ability to find out not only what people are thinking but also discover the intention behind their actions is absolutely unique. Certainly none of my dragons can do that."

"Then we have Rastan, with weather magic," added Blossom, "which is really unique. He's also telepathic and has minor telekinetic abilities, but the weather magic is something I've never heard of. Esme's gift is probably a variant or enhancement of telepathy, but the weather magic isn't related to any magic we know of. Jasper is not only telepathic but apparently developing telekinesis as well."

"Precisely," said Sapphire. "So where is all this coming from?"

"I remember," said Blossom, "hearing tales of how today's dragons developed from an earlier race, the Ribendi. Do we know anything about them?"

"I think there's a lot we don't know, and maybe if we understood more it might help us figure out what to do with Rastan," said Sapphire. "We need to know more about the Ribendi and how we are related to them."

"We also need to understand why humans turned on dragons and banished them to the aerie," said Ty.

What resources do we have to research this history? asked Wilhelmina.

"There are archives here that dragons have kept for centuries. Blossom and I can look into them. Well, at least we can when we aren't digging out from more snow," said Sapphire.

"I think Criseda and I should fly to the capital and talk to King Bertram about Rastan," said Ty. "And I will also try to find out what Aloysius might have in his archives. As the palace historian, he does have access to a lot of information, and I'm sure you all remember how helpful he was in trying to figure out what The Wraith was."

With those decisions made, the meeting broke up. Sapphire and Blossom returned to the aerie to search the dragon archives, and Ty and Criseda headed for the capital and King Bertram.

▲

Ty and Criseda landed in the palace courtyard in early afternoon. It seemed strange not to see mounds and mounds of snow. As they entered the castle, Ty said, "I wonder just how far Rastan's range is."

"That's a great question," said Criseda, "and I really hope that it's not increasing, the way Paul's telepathy is."

Henry, the castle steward, answered their knock. "Ty, Criseda, it's so good to see you. Are you here to speak with King Bertram?"

"Yes, Henry," said Ty, "if he's free."

"I'm sure he is. We've been hearing strange rumors about events in Dragonwind. But let me just check." Henry left them in the castle entryway and went to find King Bertram.

He returned a few minutes later and said, "The king would be delighted to see you both. Please follow me."

Henry led them to King Bertram's study. The palace corridors and doorways were wide enough to accommodate Criseda without difficulty. Once they reached the king's study door, Henry knocked, opened the door, and announced them. He was a stickler for protocol, and Ty respected that.

Once they were in King Bertram's office, the king, a tall, slim man in his late thirties, said, "Ty, have a seat, and Criseda, please make yourself comfortable."

Once everyone was settled, Bertram said, "What's this I've been hearing about record snowfall?"

Ty and Criseda both groaned, and Ty said, "*Snow* has gotten to be a really dirty word around Dragonwind. Have you heard of a weather mage named Rastan?"

"No, I haven't."

"Well, he's determined to get rid of the dragons and retake most of the land around Dragonwind and the aerie. He says all that land belonged to his ancestors centuries ago. He thinks he has the strongest magic, stronger even than dragons."

"That's quite a claim," said Bertram. "Is there any truth in it?"

"He's certainly powerful. He's been causing earthquakes and tremendous snowstorms, both on the aerie and in Dragonwind. We've gotten snow nearly every day for the last month, and there are still two more months of winter.

If he keeps up at this rate, we'll get about nine times our normal annual snowfall."

"Gads," said Bertram.

"For sure," said Ty. "We do have a day off after about every four to five days of snow. Wilhelmina says that's when he switches his location, and Sapphire thinks that he also needs to rest after such an expenditure of magical energy. So he does have limits, but certainly none of us, dragon, animal, or human, can do what he's doing."

"How can I help?" asked Bertram. "Clearly this Rastan has to be stopped."

"For sure," said Ty. "We've been talking about how the dragons came to be here, how they've interacted with humans, and whether the amount of magic in our world is increasing. We're also trying to figure out if there are different kinds of magic—dragon, human, nonhuman, for instance. What I'd like to do is talk to Aloysius and see if he has any ancient records that might help us figure things out."

"I'd be interested in that as well," said Bertram. "Let's go talk with him. Criseda, I'm afraid the circular stairway to Aloysius's archives is definitely not dragon friendly. But while we're with him, would you like to visit my children? They're always so happy to see you."

"It would be my honor, sire," said Criseda, causing Bertram to blink.

"You can use our speech," he said in surprise.

"Yes," said Criseda. "We've always been able to but chose not to for, I'm afraid, very arrogant reasons. This crisis has caused us to rethink a lot of things. Where will I find the boys and the twins?"

Bertram chuckled and said, "At this point in the afternoon, I believe they are all out on the back lawn. Do you know your way?"

"Certainly," said Criseda as she left Bertram's office.

▲

As Bertram and Ty climbed the steep spiral staircase, Bertram said, "I suspect that there's more to this story than you've told me."

"Yes," said Ty. "I don't know that I've left out anything major, but there have been some interesting developments, including the fact that we think Rastan is worried that his son, Jasper, who's two years younger than Prince

Raymond and whom Rastan has been abusing for years, may have stronger magic than he does. Jasper's magic is just starting to develop, but he has not only telepathic skills but also telekinetic talents. In addition, he's formed a true empathetic bond with a newly hatched dragon, Bergamen, who is the son of Windsong and Ventus, two dragons who had been living independently, away from the aerie, because they felt there should be more dragon-human interactions. Unfortunately, Rastan killed both of them, but not before Windsong was able to instruct Bergamen while he was in his egg. Jasper saved Bergamen's life, and now they're both living with Martha in Dragonwind."

"Gads, that's a lot to process," said King Bertram.

"For sure," said Ty. "I'd like you to meet Jasper and Bergamen. They're quite a pair. But right now Rastan is continuing a telepathic assault on them both, so we're doing our best to protect them. Wilhelmina is a big help with that, as she's definitely the strongest telepath on the planet, and she's able to listen in on Rastan's abuse, although he doesn't realize that."

They reached the top of the stairs and knocked on Aloysius's door before opening it and walking in.

"Hi, Aloysius," said Ty. "I need your help in researching the ancient relationships between dragons and humans."

The old man looked up from his desk. "Ancient history…hmm. Yes, that would be very ancient. Do you have a reason?"

Ty smiled and nodded. "We have an evil mage named Rastan to stop, and he's demonstrating a new kind of magic. It seems that he can control the weather, at least within a limited range. This is not magic that either the dragons or other humans can do. When we were discussing it and trying to figure out how to stop him, Blossom, one of the oldest dragons, started talking about an ancient race of dragons who predated the current dragons. I believe they were called the Ribendi.

"Sapphire also told us about why today's dragons live in the aerie, how they were kicked out of our cities by humans," concluded Ty. "We want to know as much as we can about all that to see if it could help us with our current crisis."

"Hmm," said Aloysius as he ran his hand through his white hair, causing it to be even more untidy. "I understand. Don't the dragons have records of all this?"

"Yes, we hope so," said Ty. "However, I suspect we'll get a very different perspective from any records you might have, and we need as much information as we can garner."

Aloysius chuckled, rubbing his chin. "Yes, definitely history does depend on who's telling it. It shouldn't, at least not the basics, but it always does. Well, let's see what I can find for you."

Aloysius began shifting scrolls and pieces of parchment, looking for what he needed. Finally, he said, "Here we go. This is the history of Estrea as written by Tobias nearly five hundred years ago. He says that the dragons come from an ancient lineage dating back to, as you said, the Ribendi. He goes on to detail that the dragons had the ability to talk mind to mind, what we know as telepathy."

Aloysius kept reading and finally said, "When humans first came across the dragons, they were really impressed with them. Tobias says that they were very intelligent and that they helped humans to build more complex structures. Apparently at the time, our ancestors were living in huts in a rather primitive style. The dragons were able to learn our ancestors' language very quickly, after which they spoke aloud to them, just as we do to each other.

"Our ancestors learned a lot about the land and how to survive from the dragons, and for several centuries they got along really well. However, in the time of Tobias's grandfather, things changed. Tobias says that his grandfather told him that the humans realized the dragons weren't as smart as they were. Apparently they decided they'd been fooled by the dragons, who actually were no more than advanced animals. Tobias's grandfather felt that the dragons had tricked them into doing work for the dragons, because after all, humans have hands with thumbs, and the dragons only have claws.

"Tobias doesn't seem to agree with his grandfather, or others of the time. Tobias says that humans became power hungry and that they were afraid of the dragons' magic. They were afraid of telepathy and saw it as evil. They told the dragons that they were no longer welcome, and several dragons were actually slaughtered, with great feasts given in honor of the killers—Tobias's term—as they ate the meat of the dead dragons. A few humans tried to stop the slaughter, but with no success.

"The dragons retreated to an aerie at the top of the mountain where Dragonwind is now located, and they've stayed there ever since. What a tragic story," Aloysius concluded.

"It's horrible," said Bertram. "The dragons did their best to help human-kind, and they did so much to advance human civilization, and the humans just turned on them. How could they?"

"I'm afraid," said Aloysius, "it's the same old story of fear of anything that's different, followed by a quest for power and domination."

"It sounds like what Rastan is doing now," said Ty. "How can these cycles keep repeating themselves, endlessly, time after time? Is there no hope? But this explains why Sapphire has been so reluctant to help us unless the planet or other species are in danger. After all, why should she help those who'd turned on her race so cruelly?"

"Certainly," said Aloysius. "And I believe you also asked about the Ribendi? Tobias mentions them as a race of really early dragons who adapted and became the modern dragons. It seems that the Ribendi did not have any magic, but they were very smart, and they figured out how to survive on this planet before it was tamed. I guess originally this planet was very inhospitable until first the Ribendi, and later dragons and humans, subdued it and began farming the land, planting crops, and eventually mining and logging."

"So humankind owes the dragons, and before them the Ribendi, for building our civilization. Before that we were little more than hunters and gatherers," said Ty.

"That's about it," said Aloysius. "Tobias was mortified by what his grand-father and others had done. I have other histories here, ones that are nowhere near as accurate as Tobias's, and of course they tell a different story. They talk about how violent the dragons were and how humans were only defending themselves from cruel predators. Tobias is the only one who tells what I con-sider to be the truth. His accounts of later events demonstrate his integrity as a historian, so I believe him over the others."

"I thank you, Aloysius," said Ty. "You've never steered me wrong, and what you say fits with the situation we now find ourselves in. I doubt that

Rastan has read any history, and I also doubt that he finds any need to justify his actions, but what he's doing, in addition to the weather magic, is trying to kill all dragons. I suspect after that he plans to go after anyone who stands in his way of claiming all the land around Dragonwind..."

"Others might have something to say about that," chuckled Bertram.

"Tobias notes that the aerie and the land that Dragonwind now occupies had belonged to several wealthy families, but that when the dragons took over the mountaintop, those families left. I guess it's possible that this Rastan is a descendant of one of those families," said Aloysius.

"According to Jasper, his father is determined to take over all that land. He can really wreak havoc with the weather. He already has the power to cause heavy flooding in the spring, which could prevent the sowing of crops; severe drought in the summer, which would kill any crops even if they had gotten planted; storms in the fall so anything that had somehow managed to survive couldn't be harvested; and you have heard about our winter, with nine times the amount of snow as usual. I think unless we start planning now, Rastan has the power to bring us to our knees as our food supplies vanish before us, forcing us to abandon the land," said Ty.

"That's quite a picture you're painting," said Bertram. "Is he really that powerful?"

"At the moment his range seems to be limited," said Ty, "as witnessed by the fact that you aren't buried under several feet of snow here. But that raises another question. We've noticed that the amount of magic on this planet seems to be growing. You yourself, sire, have gained a lot of strength in your ability to use telepathy. We're watching Jasper's magic develop at a very rapid rate. More animals, such as foxes, cats, squirrels, bears, and so forth, are able to communicate with us telepathically. None of us know where this increase in magic is coming from. And now Tobias's writings tells us that the Ribendi did not have magical abilities at all. Did they develop magic as they evolved into dragons? How did magic arrive in our world? We know that the dragons developed telepathy. What other magic did they learn? Is this growth in magic something that the planet is doing? And if so, why? We need to find out, because if Rastan's power is growing, he might be able to extend his range. That would certainly bring us to our knees."

"But surely this isn't possible," said Bertram.

"I wouldn't like to take a chance. We need to believe that it is and find a way to stop him," said Ty.

"Obviously, anything that I can do, I'll do," said Bertram.

"We don't want history to repeat itself," said Aloysius. "I think it's important to note that while the dragons had every reason to retaliate against our ancestors, they chose not to. They retreated to the aerie, where they've lived separate, peaceful lives, causing no harm to those who turned on them. That doesn't happen among humans. If someone wrongs us, we tend to strike back. We saw that with a vengeance when The Wraith was influencing our most powerful leaders. Your solution, Ty, was worthy of the dragons. Let's hope we can do it again."

"Thanks, Aloysius," said Ty. "I don't know why people can't learn that more can be done with cooperation and understanding than violence. We're going to need a lot of it if we're going to survive what Rastan is trying to do."

"Do you have any ideas?" asked Bertram.

"I'm starting to get some," said Ty. "I think Jasper's knowledge of his father is the best chance we have. Jasper said that his father was limited by the actual seasons. In other words, he can't make a drought in the winter, for example. So we know what he's likely to do. I need to meet with Wilson and the other craftsmen in Dragonwind. I think we're going to need a way to save water, and even snow that will melt into water, and store it so we have it for the drought we know is going to come. I haven't figured out how we'll get crops planted, but if we do manage that, we have to be able to keep them alive and healthy. Those are the only thoughts I have at the moment. I'll keep you posted, but now I think Criseda and I had better head back to Dragonwind. I'm sure there's more snow to deal with."

CHAPTER 10

PLANNING

Ty and Criseda had lots to ponder as they flew back to Dragonwind. Ty said, "So what do you think now about our partnership? Are you jealous of what Bergamen and Jasper have?"

"A little," said Criseda. "What about you?"

"I guess," said Ty. "It's so clear that the two of them belong together. But so do we, don't we?"

"Definitely," answered Criseda. "I hadn't realized how much I depend on you until Sapphire forbade any contact. Even when I was up at the aerie, we were always connected telepathically."

"For sure," said Ty. "I couldn't do anything when you were shut away from me. I depend on you as well. And we have become nearly the same as Bergamen and Jasper, I think. We don't function when we are apart."

"I think Sapphire has realized that, and she, at least tacitly, has given her permission for me to leave the aerie to be with you all the time. I think the crisis has made it clear that Windsong and Ventus were right. The dragons should never have become so isolated, although I certainly understand why that happened."

"I think they must have been very hurt when the humans turned on them after all the dragons had done for humankind," said Ty. "Calling them dumb animals was the lowest blow."

"But now we need to regroup and look at the world differently," said Criseda. "We need to work together, regardless of species, to keep this planet safe from any threats. Remember our conflict with The Wraith. If we hadn't had Rupert and Samantha and all their friends watching out for Esme, things might have gone very differently."

"That's certainly true," said Ty. "Hey, if you aren't going to live in the aerie, where are we going to live?"

"I've been thinking about that," said Criseda. "Your cave is too small, and my cave is in the aerie. Do you think we could find another larger cave on Dragonwind's outskirts? I really can't see living in a human house, although Wilhelmina has adapted well to Naomi and Paul's home, which of course they designed with her in mind."

"True," said Ty, "but Paul has only just turned seven and so really needs to be with his mother. Our situation is quite different. I think we should look for a suitable cave. Maybe Kyle would help. He used to be a hermit in the environs around Dragonwind. Jeb might also know of a place from his work as forest manager."

"Sounds good," said Criseda. "I think we can be happy in Dragonwind. The villagers were afraid of me in the beginning, but face it, now they have a number of unusual teams living in their midst. There's Paul and Wilhelmina, and Esme with Rupert and Samantha, as well as us. I think that's a good thing."

"So do I," said Ty. "We're nearly at Dragonwind now. I'm going to ask Sapphire to join us, and Blossom, if she isn't already here, so we can share what we've learned with everyone and then form a plan."

▲

It was late afternoon when they landed and discovered that Blossom was indeed in Dragonwind. She and Wilhelmina were working with Bergamen and Jasper. Sapphire joined them at Ty's request. Paul, Esme, Martha, Kyle, and Wilson completed the group, which gathered in the village hall, where they could eat dinner while they discussed what they'd learned.

Ty began by sharing the ancient history from Tobias's writings. Sapphire and Blossom nodded as he explained how the dragons had been banished.

Sapphire said, "The dragons, according to our records, were really hurt by the ingratitude of the humans. They vowed never again to get involved with them. However, they didn't abandon the entire planet. They still looked after all the other species, and as we know, they did step in when there was a problem with humankind that would affect the entire planet adversely."

"I guess we can see where you were coming from," said Ty, "and we should all be very grateful that you did offer assistance on several occasions in spite of the way our ancestors treated you. I, for one, understand your decisions a lot better in view of this information."

Sapphire dipped her head in acknowledgment.

Ty continued. "In light of this new knowledge, I've realized that none of us has any idea why Rastan is doing what he's doing. Why does he feel he has to reclaim his family's ancient lands, and why does he hate the dragons so much? Is there any chance he's been badly treated, and we can repair relations with him? Jasper, do you know anything of your father's history?"

"Not a lot," answered Jasper. "I do remember him telling me on several occasions that nobody could be trusted, that everyone lied. He also found some really old family journals, and he seemed to think that his family used to be really rich and powerful but that they lost that power because of the dragons. Also, I guess he was the only one in his family to have any magic, and he was beaten badly every time he used his telekinesis. Then when he also developed weather magic, his family expected him to change the weather to benefit their crops. But they never thanked him. I got the idea that they just took advantage of him when it suited them, and otherwise they teased and abused him."

"So not a happy childhood, for sure," said Ty. "But neither you nor Esme had a happy childhood, yet you're both warm, caring, kind individuals."

"We don't really know what kind of a person Rastan is," said Esme.

"That's true," said Ty. "Is there any way that you can discover more about him, Esme?"

It was Wilhelmina who answered. *I was meaning to let you know what I want to try. As you know, I'm trying to help Jasper learn to block his father's telepathy. What I'd like to try is to have both Jasper and Esme—well, for the lack of a better term—piggyback onto my telepathic search for Rastan. I want Jasper to see inside his father's mind to show*

Jasper how he might block Rastan. And I want Esme to be able to do just as you suggest, to discover Rastan's past and his true intentions.

"Do you really think you can do this?" asked Sapphire.

Honestly, I'm not sure, said Wilhelmina. We've tried some piggybacking telepathic journeys already, but with friends. We managed it with Rupert, Samantha, and Blossom. So I'm hopeful.

Sapphire said, "It's worth a try."

Criseda added, "I've been thinking about our thoughts on magic and how it seems to be changing, with more magic and different kinds of magic. But something occurred to me when Ty and I were with King Bertram. You may recall how we said that his telepathy was a lot stronger. Well, it is, but is that because of more magic, or is it a matter of his needing it more and using it more? After all, when someone exercises, they get stronger."

"That's true," said Kyle. "So you're thinking that if King Bertram hadn't needed better telepathic communications, he wouldn't have changed."

"Yes," said Criseda. "And the same can be said for Paul. He was responsive to Wilhelmina out of a real need to save his friends who were forced into the mines. When he came here, he met Esme, and I'm sure his desire to be with her and be part of the group caused him to strengthen his skills so he could keep up with Rupert, Samantha, and, of course, Esme."

"If I'm understanding you properly," said Sapphire, "the changes we're seeing in the strengths of individual magic is more a matter of magical creatures, including humans, actually using the talents that they have been born with. If we hadn't had these various crises, then Paul might never have realized he was telepathic, and the same with King Bertram, and possibly even many of the animals as well."

"Precisely," said Criseda.

"OK," said Blossom, "but what about Esme's unique talent of being able to discern motives and intentions, not to mention Rastan's weather magic?"

Wilhelmina said, *I've always suspected that Esme's gift is strong telepathy and that linked to that is her own ability to empathize with others. Telepathy and empathy combined, not to mention her own innate ability to read people, make her able to do what she does. It's not a new form of magic, just a rare combination of magic and other gifts.*

And then we have Jasper. He's always been telepathic, but practice and necessity have been strengthening his talent. I'm sure that he's also had the gift for telekinesis, but it only surfaced when he was threatened. After all, Ty, you have two gifts and always have, telepathy and healing. I'm sure you'll agree that both of those talents have gotten stronger as you practiced them.

"Fair enough," said Ty, "but what about Rastan? I've never heard of weather magic before."

Martha chuckled and said, "Oh, yes, we all have. Throughout history there have always been so-called witches who could make it rain. I suspect that they had weather magic. They just didn't realize it or care to abuse it. Anyone with half a brain could see that dabbling in weather magic is potentially very dangerous. What if you started something you couldn't stop?"

Sapphire said, "Martha's correct. I hadn't thought of it that way before, but it might be that the increase in both types and amounts of magic isn't due to some new influx of magical energy but rather to the changing times and various challenges that we've had to face, which have allowed us to exercise our use of magic for the good of all."

"Well, Rastan isn't using it for the good of all," said Blossom.

"True," said Sapphire. "So we're back to trying to understand his motivation."

I'll take responsibility for trying to discover that, with Esme and Jasper's help, said Wilhelmina.

Wilson spoke up for the first time. "I think I'm following much of this, but my real question is, what are we going to do to protect ourselves if Rastan can't be reasoned with?"

Ty nodded and said, "That's a very important question. First, we are fairly sure that after the record snows of winter, we'll be enduring record rains of spring, followed by a summer drought. Is that what you predict, Jasper, based on your knowledge of your father and his talents?"

"Yes," said Jasper, "I'm afraid so."

"I have a suggestion about preparing for all that," said Ty. "We need to build reservoirs that can hold the tremendous spring rains and then have irrigation lines so that we can water crops and have water for us through the summer drought. Wilson, what do you think? Can you and the other villagers manage something along those lines?"

"Well, yes," said Wilson. "I think we can. And we might also be able to rig up some sort of canopy over the growing areas. We're lucky, actually, that Dragonwind has such poor soil, so that most of our food comes from trading lumber and precious metals for food and cloth. We only have a few gardens where fresh veggies are grown, and I think we can take care of them as you suggest, Ty."

"Good," said Ty. "Then we need to figure out how to stop Rastan. I'm not sure I have any answers for that, but I do know that Rastan is afraid of Jasper's abilities."

At this Jasper spluttered, "He's afraid of *me*?"

"Yes, and to be honest, I've wondered why," said Ty. "But now I think I know. We've said that magical gifts are present at birth. What if when you were an infant or small child, you demonstrated your telekinetic talent? You might not even remember it, and certainly your father wouldn't remind you of it, if I'm thinking correctly about a way to challenge him."

"What's that?" asked Jasper.

"Have you and Criseda or Blossom been working on your telekinesis?"

"A bit," said Jasper.

"I want that to be a major focus now," said Ty. "I want you to start by helping with all our snow, not with a shovel but with your telekinetic powers. I want to develop your telekinetic muscles, so to speak, so that you can move mounds of snow."

"But what good will that be?" asked Jasper.

Esme was all but bouncing up and down, because she saw just where Ty was going. "You think he'll be able to move storms away from Dragonwind."

Ty smiled and said, "Yes, Esme. That's my hope. If your telekinesis is strong enough, I want you to push storm clouds away. And you won't have to push them a great distance."

"The old mining towns," said Paul, catching on as well.

"Yes, Paul," said Ty. "Those old towns are now abandoned after all the mine collapses, so there's no one to be hurt by the storms. If Jasper can nudge the clouds away from Dragonwind and the aerie and send them to the mining towns, then Rastan's purposes will be defeated."

"At least for a bit," said Sapphire. "I suspect he'll move on to other areas where Jasper isn't, or else he'll try to capture or kill Jasper."

"Point taken," said Ty. "This isn't a final solution by any means. I don't have any idea what that final solution might be. But at least we have something to be going on with. Wilson and his crew will design reservoir tanks and canopies. Wilhelmina will try, with Esme and Jasper's help, to figure out what makes Rastan tick. And Jasper will learn to move a lot of snow and start to try moving storm clouds."

Sapphire said, "That's certainly an excellent start to our defense. Finding Rastan would also help. I could do a lot if I could see him, but I can't help much unless I can look him in the eyes."

Wilhelmina said, *I've been trying to find his hiding spots, but so far, without any luck. The minute I get close, he vanishes. But I'll keep working on it.*

Bergamen said softly, "I understand the plan, but you do realize that a lot of this rests on Jasper and that he'll be an even bigger target for Rastan. I'm getting a lot bigger, and my wing has healed," he said, puffing out his chest. He was now nearly as large as a very large dog.

"However, I'm not full grown, and I'm certainly no match for a fight with Rastan."

Ty looked over at the young dragon, who certainly was growing quickly on Martha's food. "Don't worry, Bergamen. We will take no chances with Jasper. His safety, as well as yours, is of paramount importance to us all."

With that the meeting ended, and everyone headed off to bed. They would begin their plan in the morning.

CHAPTER 11

ANGER

In the morning a group of villagers confronted Ty at the village hall. The leader of the group, a man named Gorst, said, "We need to talk with you. We're tired of all this snow. It isn't right."

"I know," said Ty. "We're all tired of it."

"You don't understand," Gorst went on. "The only reason we have all this snow is because of that brat and his baby dragon that you're keeping here. He doesn't belong here. With his dark skin, he doesn't look anything like us. And we certainly don't need another weird pairing in this village. We have you and your dragon, that other boy and his moose, and that strange girl with a fox and a squirrel. And you aren't even a real man. This village is getting out of hand, and now we have way too much snow. They need to go, and we need to get this village back to the way it was."

His fellow villagers nodded their agreement. Ty looked at them all and said, "So how long have you been feeling this way?"

"A long time," said Gorst. "But this snow is the last straw. We won't have it."

"I see," said Ty. "Well we'd better have a village meeting to discuss this and see how many other villagers feel this way."

"We don't need another meeting where you can perform your magic and get folks to agree," said Gorst. "We need at least the mage's son gone. Then the mage will stop making it snow every two minutes."

"I'm not going to banish anyone without a fair hearing. Tomorrow morning at ten o'clock, we'll have everyone meet here in the village hall, and you can present your case. That's my final word. I will not make such a decision without the villagers' input," said Ty.

After the men left, Ty headed out to find Martha and Kyle. He figured they'd know what was going on.

When Ty had left, Jasper and Bergamen came out from a side room. "Did you hear all that?" said Jasper.

"Yes," said Bergamen.

"We're causing problems for our new friends," said Jasper.

"And you know they're never going to agree to kick us out," said Bergamen.

"What that man said is true," said Jasper. "We're the cause of all this snow, or at least I am. I need to leave before I cause more problems for everyone."

"You aren't going without me," said Bergamen.

"You'd also be better off without me," said Jasper.

"Not going to happen," said Bergamen firmly.

"OK, but we need to be quick. I'll grab some food and put on all my warmest clothing, and then we'll leave out the back way."

▲

It didn't take long for Jasper and Bergamen to gather their few things and head out. They took back paths, away from any homes, and headed in the direction of the old mining towns. It was hard going once they were outside the village, because they had to trudge their way through the deep snow. Thankfully, the last few days had been cold enough to freeze the top layer, so they weren't sinking deeply into the snow. It helped that both of them were light in weight.

They'd been walking for a couple hours and were getting very tired when it started to snow again. It was snowing really hard, and soon it was difficult to see where they were going. Then the voice Jasper dreaded hearing said, *Did you think I wasn't watching you? You and that runt of a dragon will die out here, and that suits me fine. You'll be trapped in a blizzard. There will be no getting out, and your so-called friends won't be able to find you until it's too late.*

Jasper sank to his knees and said to Bergamen, "Do you think he's right? Are we going to die?"

Bergamen said, "I don't know, but we have to keep trying. Come on, let's see if we can find somewhere to shelter. There has to be a cave of some kind around here."

"At least our friends are safe now," said Jasper. "We're far enough away from Dragonwind that this snowstorm can't touch them. If we do die, then my father will leave them alone."

"Maybe," said Bergamen. "He does want to reclaim all the land around here, though, so he's going to have to go after humans as well as dragons."

"I guess," said Jasper, "but at least it won't be my fault."

"None of this is your fault," said Bergamen. "I wish you'd believe that. We're each of us only responsible for our own actions."

Jasper shrugged, and the two of them trudged onward. They wandered lost for nearly thirty minutes before they finally found a small alcove to shelter in. Jasper opened his pack and got out a couple of pieces of dried meat, one for each of them. They were exhausted, and soon both of them fell asleep.

▲

Meanwhile, back in Dragonwind, Esme ran to find Ty. She found him talking with Martha and Kyle. Jeb walked up to them just as Esme ran up to say, "Bergamen and Jasper are gone!"

"Gone?" said Martha with dismay in her voice.

Ty looked at Esme and said, "Where have they gone?"

"They left Dragonwind, and I think they are headed to the abandoned mining towns," said Esme. "Jasper overheard some men saying that all of Dragonwind's problems are because of him and he needs to be made to leave."

"We'd never send them away," said Ty.

"They know that, but when I looked into Jasper's mind, it was clear that he feels guilty for bringing his father's wrath on the village. You have all been so good to him, and he's only repaid you with one disaster after another. Jasper thinks that if they leave—and he did try to persuade Bergamen to stay here, but of course he wouldn't have that—if they leave, then the snow will stop, and life in Dragonwind can get back to what we had before."

"We have to find them," said Criseda. "They won't last the night out there, especially if Rastan brings more snow."

Wilhelmina joined the group then and said, *I just heard Rastan taunting Jasper. It appears that Jasper and Bergamen are lost in a blizzard, some two hours from here, and Rastan is sure he's going to kill him with this latest snowstorm. He seems very happy about it all. We need to find them.*

"OK," said Ty. "Criseda and I will fly toward the abandoned mining villages. Wilhelmina, can you track them and keep us posted?"

Yes, answered Wilhelmina. *I'll get outside the village and head along the route I think they took. I'll also try to contact them to let them know that help is on the way.*

"I tried to reach them," said Esme, panic rising in her voice, "but I couldn't make contact."

"We'll find them," said Ty. "We just have to. We have about three hours before it's dark."

Paul was standing beside Wilhelmina, looking terrified. "I thought I'd die when my friends and I were trapped in the mine collapse. You, Ty, and Wilhelmina, you found us. Do you think you can find Jasper and Bergamen? Oh, why did they do something so foolish?"

"Because," said Esme, her voice trembling, "because they love us and are grateful to us, and they don't want to cause us any harm. I do understand why Jasper felt he had to leave. I felt the same way when The Wraith and my parents were after me. The only reason I didn't run for it was because I was too injured to get out of bed for the longest time, and then, by the time I could have run, I was being taught by the dragons, and I realized I could be more help in catching The Wraith if I stayed right where I was.

"But there's a big difference between my case and Jasper's. I was the only one in danger from The Wraith. I was the one he wanted. I was the one with the magical gift to understand people's thoughts and intentions. Jasper's father is harming both the aerie and all of Dragonwind. He's making life miserable for everyone, not just Jasper or even Jasper and Bergamen. I know Jasper was foolish, but his heart's in the right place, and I definitely understand why he's doing what he feels he has to do to protect everyone else."

"He's certainly nothing like his father," said Kyle.

Ty jumped onto Criseda's back and said, "We will bring both of them back, safe and sound. Wilhelmina, let us know if you discover anything."

Will do, said Wilhelmina.

It wasn't long before Ty sent a telepathic message back. *We've just run into a blizzard. Jasper was right that his father's range is limited. Rastan is definitely targeting his son. At least this blizzard won't reach Dragonwind, which would only give Gorst and his buddies ammunition for getting Jasper and Bergamen out of Dragonwind. Wilhelmina, can you find them? Criseda and I can't see a thing in this blizzard. I'm not getting any answer from my telepathic calls either.*

I'm not finding them anywhere. And I'm also not getting any answers.

Criseda and I are going to land and try to make our way on foot. We are in the center of the blizzard, which must mean we're close, as Rastan would be centering the storm over them. We'll let you know if we find them.

Criseda landed, and the two of them walked through the deepest snows, looking for anywhere that might offer shelter to the two small creatures. They also called out to any animals who might be in the area.

Ty and Criseda headed in opposite directions and then set up a circular pattern, figuring that they would cover more ground with greater efficiency. As they circled, they continued to move toward the abandoned mines. They'd been searching for an hour when Ty heard crying.

Criseda, over here. Someone's crying. I think it's Bergamen. We need to dig here.

It wasn't long before Criseda said, *I've found a very small overhang, and I think they are under it. I'm digging carefully, since I don't know just where they are inside, and I don't want to dig into them.*

Ty raced over to help, using his hands to gently move snow away from a couple of small bumps. He wanted to tell Criseda to hurry, but he knew that they did have to be careful, since at least one of them was still alive. They dug through nearly five feet of snow before they found the opening to the alcove.

The rescue work then went a lot faster. They could see the entrance, and all they needed to do was clear it. Jasper and Bergamen, thankfully, weren't buried, just trapped.

Ty was right. It was Bergamen who was crying. When he saw Ty and Criseda, he said, "I can't wake him. I can't reach him."

"Hang on, Bergamen," said Ty. "Are you OK?"

"I'm so cold, but Jasper won't wake up," said Bergamen, "and he's very, *very* cold."

Ty reached for Bergamen, but Bergamen said, "No, get Jasper first. Please. Is he still alive?"

Ty lifted Jasper. He felt for a pulse and thought he might be detecting a very faint one. "I think so," said Ty. "But he's barely alive. I need to put you on Criseda and then have you hold Jasper long enough for me to get up. Then we'll put a blanket I brought around him, and I'll hold him tight to my chest for warmth as we fly back to Dragonwind. Can you do that?"

"Yes," said Bergamen with determination.

Once Ty was on Criseda, holding tight to a bundled Jasper, with Bergamen wrapping his front legs around him, Criseda took off. Immediately they were buffeted by severe winds, and they heard Rastan in their heads saying, *You'll never reach Dragonwind. I'll keep you here until Jasper is dead. You were fools to come after these two.*

Criseda tried to fly west to Dragonwind, but she wasn't making any real headway. Then they heard Wilhelmina. *Rastan, you're the fool. I've now found you. I've told Sapphire and Blossom exactly where you are. They'll be at your location in a few minutes. You have a choice. You may either keep the blizzard blowing, which will result in your capture, or you can flee again to play more of this cat-and-mouse game we've been having. Which is it?*

You can't have found my location. You're bluffing.

Rastan had no sooner said this than Ty could telepathically sense a loud trumpeting sound above the mage. He guessed that this was either Sapphire or Blossom and that Wilhelmina hadn't been bluffing after all. *I'll get you later,* Rastan shouted as he ran for a new hiding place.

The winds stopped almost immediately, allowing Criseda to fly back to Dragonwind.

Thanks, Wilhelmina, said Ty. *That was quick thinking.*

Wilhelmina laughed and said, *Especially since Sapphire and Blossom couldn't get close enough to you to help because of the blizzard. Really, Rastan isn't very bright. He was easy to fool, thankfully.*

You fooled me as well, said Ty. *Great job!*

Once Criseda reached Dragonwind, she landed in front of Martha's cottage. Martha, Kyle, Jeb, Esme, and Paul met them. Wilhelmina arrived shortly from the edge of the village, where she'd been monitoring events. Ty handed Jasper down to Martha and then gave Bergamen to Kyle.

Bergamen tried to say he could walk, but Kyle just bundled him up and carried him into Martha's home. He might have been be the size of a very large dog, but Kyle was strong and used to carrying heavy weights.

"Is he alive?" cried Bergamen again.

Both Ty and Martha worked on Jasper. Kyle said, "They're doing their best."

Jeb came into the bedroom with hot water bottles, which they placed around Jasper's still form. Ty sent every bit of healing magic he had into the boy. Martha dripped an herb concoction into his mouth. The others just waited.

Suddenly Esme said, "I can feel him."

Wilhelmina, who couldn't fit in Martha's cottage and so had to stick her head through the window, said, *So can I. He's not answering, but I, too, can feel him.*

"Why won't he answer?" said Bergamen.

Ty stumbled as he stood, and Kyle reached for him. "You need food, Ty. You've expended all your energy."

Ty barely nodded. Jeb hurried out of the room to make sandwiches and quickly returned to give some to Ty, along with a mug of hot tea.

"Thanks, Jeb," said Ty.

Martha stood and said, "He's now in a natural sleep. We should let him rest, and he'll wake up when he's ready to. But he's alive, Bergamen. With any luck, he will make a full recovery."

Bergamen started to cry tears of joy. Ty said, "Bergamen, do you realize that you saved Jasper?"

"How?" said Bergamen.

"If you hadn't cried when you thought Jasper was dying, we wouldn't have heard you. We probably would have found you eventually, but it would have been too late for Jasper."

"Oh," said Bergamen.

"And Wilhelmina, your ruse with Rastan also saved Jasper's life. He was nearly gone when we got here. If we'd been delayed any longer, he would have died before we reached Dragonwind."

I'm so glad it worked. Rastan really is a very weak, stupid man.

"OK," said Martha. "Everyone out. Well, except you, Bergamen. You and I will watch over Jasper tonight."

Bergamen said, "Thanks, Martha. And thanks to everyone who helped rescue us. We really are very glad to be back, although we're sorry that you'll be getting more snow now that we are here again."

"Don't worry about that," said Ty. "We'll find a way to stop Rastan. Now remember, you, too, need warmth, food, and sleep. Martha, I'll take a brief nap and then relieve you on watch."

CHAPTER 12

VILLAGE MEETING

First thing the next morning, Ty went to check on Jasper and Bergamen. Bergamen was sitting right on top of Jasper's bed, getting as close as possible to the boy. Jasper was still asleep. Martha said, "I think it's more than sleep. I think he's actually unconscious, because if he were just asleep, Bergamen would be able to reach him telepathically. I'm not worried yet. We brought him back from near death, and his body has a lot of healing to do."

"But he will wake up, won't he?" asked Bergamen.

"I have no reason to doubt it," said Martha.

Ty used his healing magic to check on Jasper, and after a few minutes he said, "Yes, he's unconscious, not just asleep. But I can find no major injuries, so I believe you are correct, Martha. He's been deeply traumatized, and this is his way of coping. Given that his father keeps breaking through telepathically, it would make sense that he'd go somewhere that's safe from telepathy. I'm going to ask Wilhelmina to keep a telepathic shield around Jasper so that Rastan can't break in. That should provide the security that Jasper needs. We'll see if it helps him to wake up."

Bergamen nodded with understanding. Then he said, "Does Wilhelmina have to block all telepathy, or can she block just Rastan?"

"I'll ask her," said Ty, "and I'll have her let you know. Meanwhile, you also need to rest."

Ty motioned to Martha, and the two of them stepped out of the room. "Are you going to be able to leave them to come to the village meeting?"

"I've asked Esme and Paul to sit with Jasper and Bergamen during the meeting," said Martha. "I can't believe that many villagers support Gorst and his friends; at least I hope not."

"Thanks," said Ty.

Two hours later the village hall was filled with people. It looked as if the entire village had showed up, which pleased Ty. No matter how things went, at least they'd have a definite decision this morning.

Ty called the meeting to order. Once everyone had quieted, he said, "Yesterday a delegation came to me, claiming to represent the village and saying that I needed to send Jasper and Bergamen away. I called this meeting because even though I'm the mayor as well a roving ambassador for King Bertram, I didn't feel that I should make the decision without a vote from everyone."

This statement produced an undercurrent of muttering, but Ty couldn't say whether it was for or against the idea or some combination.

"In addition, they said that they didn't like the new influx of strange magical pairings. They mentioned specifically Criseda and me, Esme with Rupert and Samantha, and Paul and Wilhelmina. The spokesperson called us *freaks* who weren't needed."

This now caused an uproar, and someone in the back said, "You mean *Gorst* said that!"

Ty held up a hand for quiet. "Before we do anything else, I'd like to tell you what happened yesterday after the delegation left."

The room got very quiet. Ty then said, "It turns out that Jasper and Bergamen overheard what the delegation said. As soon as I left the hall, they packed up their few belongings and headed out. Bergamen said that Jasper didn't want to cause problems for those who'd been so kind to them. He's very aware that it's his father who is causing all the snow.

"So this brave young man and his small dragon left Dragonwind and tried to make their way to the deserted mining villages. You all know how hard it is to move with all this snow, especially once you are outside the village, but this small pair felt they had to leave to protect all of you.

"Thankfully, Esme discovered what was happening. She told me and Criseda, and we headed out immediately to try to find them. You might have thought that would be easy, because we did not have a snowstorm here yesterday. But the reason that we didn't have a storm was because Rastan was following his son's progress, and he centered a blizzard right over him.

"Jasper and Bergamen became lost in the blizzard. Bergamen said they struggled in the blizzard for a long time before they found a small cave to shelter in. But then the storm completely blocked them in, covering the entrance to the cave. Rastan told them they would die there.

"And they would have—certainly Jasper would have—if Criseda and I, who had to walk the area since the blizzard was too strong to fly in, hadn't heard Bergamen crying. He thought Jasper was dead, and in fact, he nearly was. We uncovered their small cave and flew the two of them back here. It took all the skill that Martha and I have to bring Jasper back, and even now he's still unconscious. We're hoping he'll make a full recovery, but we aren't certain yet."

Ty looked around the room. No one said a word. Finally Ty said, "What I'd like to know is, how can those of you who wanted to shove this brave pair out of here live with yourselves? Jasper did what none of you were brave enough to do. He left to protect you, you who have done nothing to help either him or Bergamen.

"And what have Jasper and Bergamen been doing since this snow started? How many of you have they helped? How many paths have they shoveled? And now they're going to try to increase their magical talents by moving the snow with telekinesis. Maybe you think it would be easier just to shovel the snow, but he's going to try to do it magically, and why? Have any of you asked why Jasper wants to do it that way? It's because he's trying to increase his abilities so that he can move the actual storm clouds away from the village and keep the snow far from us.

"It seems to me that those villagers you want to get rid of are the same villagers who've helped above and beyond what anyone else is able to do. No one has moved more snow than Wilhelmina. Esme has been able to follow Rastan's movements enough to know when the next storm will hit and give us a heads-up. Rupert and Samantha have been checking each and every home in Dragonwind to be sure no one is forgotten or trapped. No one asked them to do all this. They did it because they care about the village and everyone in it."

Ty turned to Gorst and his buddies and said, "I haven't seen any of you helping anyone but yourselves. Jasper and Bergamen's actions put you to shame. You wanted them gone, but do you realize that Jasper's father killed his mother when Jasper was only five? Rastan then killed first Bergamen's father and later his mother. These two have nowhere else to go. They have no family. They have been trying to make us their family. You nearly cost them their lives."

Ty then looked around the room. "I know the snow is difficult, but what I'd like to know is, do Gorst and his friends speak for the majority? Do you really want all of us who are different to leave?" With that Ty sat down and waited.

No one spoke for the longest time. Finally Wilson, the carpenter, stood and spoke. "My family and I haven't lived here long, but we've been happy. We thought we'd found a good place, with good people. I've built or repaired a lot of homes for you. I had no idea that you felt this way about Ty and Criseda, who've done so much to help this village prosper, or Paul, his mother Naomi, and Wilhelmina, who've given of their time and talents as well. Esme, Rupert, and Samantha have made sure all of us stay safe time and time again. Now we have the chance to help Jasper and Bergamen, who as Ty said, are kind and generous. If you can turn on these folks, what's to say you won't turn on us? Maybe you won't like something about us. But you know what?" he said as he took his wife's hand. "We won't stay in a village that could allow this to happen. If I'd known that Jasper and Bergamen were out in that snow, I would have searched all night for them." With that he sat down.

Suddenly the room was filled with applause. There were shouts of "You're right, Wilson!" and "We're with you, Ty!"

Gorst stood and tried to speak, but he was drowned out. Finally, Ty called for silence and then said, "Gorst, did you wish to speak?"

"Yes," he said. "I stand by my words. Ty told us that we didn't get a storm last night because Jasper was away from the village. Doesn't that just prove that without him we wouldn't have all this snow? At the rate that it's falling, by the end of winter, we'll have over five hundred inches instead of our usual fifty-six. How can we handle that?"

Kyle said, "We'll find a way. Pushing Jasper and Bergamen out isn't the way to do it. It's not their fault."

Martha spoke then. "We need to pull together. If you'd been here when Criseda and Ty landed, if you'd seen how close to death those two youngsters were...and why? Because they were trying to save you—you, who abandoned them."

"I still say they need to go," said Gorst. "I didn't mean to shove them out on their own. We could find somewhere safe for them."

"Where?" asked Ty.

"I don't know," said Gorst. "Just not here."

Ty said, "OK, let's take a vote. As your mayor, I'll abide by whatever you vote for. Those who agree with Gorst and think Jasper and Bergamen should go—oh, wait, Gorst, do you also want Naomi, Paul, and Wilhelmina to go, and Esme, Rupert, and Samantha, and Criseda and me? So do you want all of us to go? If so, vote yes. If not, vote no."

Kyle handed around pieces of parchment so that the ballot would be secret, allowing everyone to vote their true feelings. He then collected the ballots, and he, Jeb, and Martha counted them. Finally, he said, "We have five-hundred twenty-seven votes here. That's the entire adult population of the village. There are four hundred ninety-six no votes and thirty-one yes."

There were loud cheers. Gorst and his friends looked disgusted. "You're siding with a bunch of freaks," he shouted over the cheering.

Kyle shook his head and said, "We're siding with our friends."

Ty called for quiet. Finally, he was able to say, "Thank you, everyone. I really hoped I hadn't misread the village's kindness my entire life. We've always stood together, and we've always helped those in need. We have survived a number of challenges, and we'll survive this one also. Together we will defeat Rastan.

"As for those who voted yes," said Ty, "you have a choice to make. You are welcome to stay if you're willing to be part of the solution. You are also welcome to leave if you find yourself uncomfortable around those you call freaks. We like our community, with all its quirks and differences. You can never say that Dragonwind is boring. If that doesn't suit you, we'll help you to find another place that will suit you better. We'll even clear a path down the mountain to get you out of the snow. The choice is yours."

Gorst and his friends stood up and left the hall. However, several of the wives from that group stayed and said, "We'd like to help, and we have children who want to help as well."

Ty nodded and said, "See Martha, and she'll get you sorted. And thanks!"

After most of the villagers had left, Ty called a meeting with Martha, Kyle, Jeb, Wilhelmina, Rupert, Samantha, and Criseda. He said, "It's true that the storms move with Jasper. I thought about going with him to the mining towns and trying to trap Rastan somehow, but I'm not sure that would work. Criseda and I could keep Jasper and Bergamen safe, but I'm guessing that Rastan would figure out that he could hurt us even more by coming after Dragonwind. We could hardly stay somewhere safe if the village was being assailed."

That's true, said Wilhelmina. She turned to Criseda and continued. *Since we have nontelepaths here, could you propose that we try our plan to use Wilhelmina, Paul, Esme, and Jasper to learn more about Rastan's motivation?*

Certainly, said Criseda before turning to the group as a whole. "Wilhelmina would like to propose that we move on with our earlier plan of trying to get inside Rastan's head and find out more about him and what his real agenda is."

Ty nodded and said, "Yes, we do need to do that, but unfortunately, we can't until Jasper is healed."

"Until then," said Jeb, "I think we should concentrate on the village buildings. Gorst wasn't wrong about the danger. We have to keep the roofs cleared, for instance. And I could use help cutting more wood. There's a lot to do to keep the village and villagers safe."

With that the meeting broke up.

CHAPTER 13

RASTAN'S PLANS

Martha kept a close watch on Jasper. She really didn't like the fact that he wasn't waking up. Wilhelmina, Esme, and Bergamen tried repeatedly to contact him telepathically to reassure him that his father couldn't reach him, but they couldn't make any contact. Blossom stopped by frequently to check on Bergamen, and she also tried to reach Jasper. In addition, she was worried about Bergamen, because he was barely eating. He was so worried about Jasper that he had no interest in anything else.

Finally, on the fourth day, Wilhelmina was able to reach Jasper telepathically, and he responded. Once she reassured him that his father couldn't get to him, he started to regain consciousness. When he opened his eyes finally, the first thing he saw was Bergamen staring at him, nearly nose to nose.

"Jasper!" Bergamen shouted. "You're awake! Finally."

Jasper just gave a weak smile. Martha left the room and returned quickly with some hot broth. "You need to eat, young man," she said as she sat down next to his bed and began feeding him.

Jasper was too weak to protest that he could feed himself. He realized that, honestly, he couldn't manage, so he let Martha take care of him. As soon as he'd finished the broth, he fell back to sleep, but this time it really was just sleep.

"Now, Bergamen," said Blossom, "you will eat a decent meal. Jasper is going to be fine, and he'll want to see how much you've grown."

"It's only been four days," protested Bergamen.

"At your age, you grow every day," said Blossom. "Now don't argue with me. I'm sure Martha has something delicious for you."

Martha laughed and said, "I do. I have a lovely rabbit stew just waiting for you. I'll be right back."

Jasper was very weak for several days. It was a full ten days before he was mostly back to his usual self. Martha and Ty didn't want him using any magic until two weeks after his rescue, and during all that time, Wilhelmina kept Rastan from reaching him.

Finally, Ty said, "OK, I think you can try some telepathy. Wilhelmina will keep you shielded from your father, but why don't you see if you can reach Esme?"

A few minutes later, Esme came racing into Jasper's bedroom. "I heard you. Are you OK now?"

"I think so," said Jasper.

Ty said, "OK, why don't you try to move your tray off the bed and over to the other side of the room? Put it on that shelf."

Jasper did as Ty requested.

"Good," said Ty. "Now do you think you can get the tray to the kitchen?"

"I think so," said Jasper, and soon, as the others watched, the tray sailed out of the bedroom.

A few minutes later, Martha came in and said, "So I don't have to pick up dirty dishes anymore? Thanks, Jasper."

▲

Over the next two weeks, Esme, Jasper, and Wilhelmina worked on setting up a piggyback network, where Jasper and Esme could follow a telepathic path that Wilhelmina set up and had ultimate control over. They practiced this system first by contacting Ty. Then they set out to contact Sapphire in the aerie. They even got good enough to contact King Bertram in the capital. They knew that the distance to King Bertram was a lot greater than the distance to Rastan.

During all this time, the snow kept piling up. Gorst and his friends had decided to leave Dragonwind, although several of the wives, including Gorst's, along with their children, stayed. Gorst's wife, Eloise, said that she would never leave Dragonwind, and honestly, she was happy to see the last of Gorst. "He only cares about himself, and he's lazy as can be. He's not interested in either me or our children. He just wants to hang around with his buddies doing nothing. I'm better off without him."

The other wives who stayed nodded in agreement. They helped each other out with the snow, and Ty made sure that Jeb and Wilson checked on them regularly, as the snow showed no sign of stopping.

Finally Wilhelmina said, *We're as ready as we can be. Let's try to get into Rastan's head. Esme, I want you to search out all the memories you can. Feel free to ransack his brain. Jasper, you just watch, and if it seems that Rastan has sensed us, then you try to distract him. Can you do that?*

"Yes," said Jasper, "as long as you're protecting us."

Don't worry, said Wilhelmina. *If needed, I can flood his mind with so much telepathic energy that it will knock him out. I'll keep both you and Esme safe. Now, are you both ready?*

They both said they were. So Wilhelmina led them into the labyrinth of Rastan's mind. Wilhelmina and Jasper just kept a waiting vigil as Esme moved around, looking for clues.

She saw a very young Rastan who was using telepathy on his mother. His mother yelled at him. The next memory showed Rastan listening to an older man who looked to be Rastan's grandfather. The grandfather was telling Rastan about his own grandfather, who had been friends with a dragon. But the dragon was killed, and then his grandfather just lost interest in everything and died shortly thereafter. Rastan's grandfather blamed the dragons for killing his own grandfather and then taking all the family lands. Rastan's grandfather said that while his grandfather had been able to communicate magically with his dragon, no one since then, until Rastan, had had any magic.

The next memory was of Rastan being thrown out of his home, with his parents shouting at him that he was never to come back. Esme thought that Rastan was about ten years old.

Then she caught glimpses of Rastan on the streets of the capital, wearing dirty and torn clothing, stealing food from various shops. He slept in parks and in alleyways.

Esme heard the young Rastan talking to himself, saying, "They'll be sorry. I'll show them. I'll be the best mage in the world. I'm powerful, and I'll get more powerful."

Esme saw a larger Rastan, who looked to be in his mid- to late teens. She watched as Rastan walked into his old home and then proceeded to kill his father, his mother, his older brother, and finally even his two younger sisters.

Next Esme saw Rastan meeting Jasper's mother at a fancy party at the palace. She was beautiful and had dark skin, just like Jasper.

As she was watching this, she felt Rastan's mind shift. Suddenly he was talking to her in real time.

So you think you can take my thoughts, do you? I know all about you, and you're weak, just like your friends.

You're a monster, said Esme. *How could you kill your entire family?*

How could I? said Rastan. *Look what they did to me. They threw me out of the house when I was ten years old. They didn't even let me pack a suitcase. I was left with nothing. How's that fair?*

I'm not saying that what they did wasn't hurtful, said Esme, *but they were scared. They didn't understand about your magic. That wasn't something that they should have been killed for.*

You don't understand, Rastan sneered. *I vowed when I left that never again would I be at anyone else's mercy. I vowed that I would take care of anyone who tried to stop me. And I have. My family was just the beginning. I've gotten rid of anyone who stood in my way. I'm the most powerful mage ever, and I'll reclaim the land that was stolen from my great-great-grandfather. I'll eliminate the dragons. I'll kill every one of them. I'll destroy Dragonwind and everyone in it. You can't stop me.*

Why did you marry? Why did you have to kill Jasper's mother?

She had magical power. Not much, but not many people do. I wanted to have a son I could train to be my apprentice, and her magics were telepathy and the ability to keep people calm. I thought that would come in handy in a son, but she tried using the calming on me to control me. She was just a miserable sandwort, yet she thought she could control me. I couldn't have that. But by then, I had Jasper ready to train.

Well, that didn't work out very well, did it? Esme taunted. *Jasper is nothing like you. He's a good and kind person, not a self-centered, power-hungry murderer.*

How dare you insult me?

Wilhelmina could feel Rastan building up an energy burst, so before he could release it, she pulled both Esme and Jasper out of the link and then blasted Rastan with a strong pulse of her own telepathic energy.

Esme and Jasper collapsed onto the couch in Martha's living room. Bergamen tried to climb into Jasper's lap, but he was really too big for that anymore. Wilhelmina called to Ty, *Can you come check that these two are OK, and also hear what we found out?*

Coming, answered Ty.

He and Criseda arrived at Martha's, and Ty, after making sure that Esme and Jasper were OK, said, "Let's go over to the village hall so Criseda can come inside. She's also contacted both Sapphire and Blossom, and they are on their way."

It didn't take long for Sapphire and Blossom to reach the village, and soon the group was gathered.

"That man is horrible," said Esme. "He is actually proud of what he's done. He's murdered a lot of people, his own parents, his brother, and two sisters. He tricked Jasper's mother into marrying him and then killed her family and eventually her, besides both of Bergamen's parents. I saw that he'd killed others as well. That seems to be his preferred way of getting rid of anyone who stands in his way."

"So I take it that there would be no way to negotiate or reason with him," said Sapphire.

"Definitely not," said Esme. "His intentions are very clear. He plans to take over both the aerie and all of Dragonwind. He says that this land be-longed to his family generations ago."

It also seems clear that he has given up on getting Jasper to cooperate, said Wilhelmina heavily.

"Oh, yes," said Esme. "When Jasper's name came up, I could read his intentions clear as day. He will kill Jasper, or at least that's what he thinks. I also read fear in his mind when he talked about Jasper. I think that he suc-ceeded in having a very magically powerful son, although obviously Jasper is just coming into his powers, but he did not, thankfully, succeed in having a son who's as big a narcissist as he is."

Bergamen moved even closer to Jasper. Jasper laid his hand on Bergamen's back, taking comfort from the contact.

Sapphire said, "So what can we do to stop this madman? We can't seem to get any closer to him, and none of our efforts to track or locate him have been successful."

"I think, for now," said Ty, "we keep on with what we've been doing. We need to keep everyone safe from the storms, and we need to help Jasper develop his powers."

"I can move snow telekinetically now," said Jasper. "I haven't succeeded with clouds, though. I'm sorry."

Ty leaned over and ruffled Jasper's hair. "Hey, you're doing an awesome job. And I want you to promise me that you won't try leaving the village. We're in this together. We need you to be safe."

Esme said, "I got a sense from Gorst that if he had a chance, he'd kidnap Jasper and turn him over to Rastan."

"That's horrible," said Criseda.

"I know," said Esme. "I'm just saying we need to be really sure we have Jasper protected, and that means that you, Jasper, have to be with one of us who can communicate telepathically at all times. You'd be partially safe with Paul, Martha, Kyle, and Jeb, but they don't have the magical skills necessary to help if someone tries to capture or kidnap you."

Ty looked at Jasper and said, "Esme is right. You are our only hope for defeating Rastan, so you must stay safe. And Rastan aside, you are our friend, and we don't want you hurt."

"But you wouldn't be in this mess if it weren't for me," said Jasper stubbornly.

"You heard him, Jasper," said Esme. "His plan is to get rid of the dragons and take over this land. Yes, he wants you dead, but even without you, the dragons are his first target, and he's already started on them, with Bergamen's parents. Then he'll move on to easier targets. He's totally insane, but he's driven to conquer. He'll kill you if he can because he's afraid of what you will become, but this isn't about you. And none of us have the ability to defeat him. You're the one he fears."

"I don't know why," said Jasper.

"Neither do we, and that's something we have to figure out. We need to find his weaknesses," said Ty.

"Do we have any idea where he is? I mean, other than the fact that he has to be reasonably close?" asked Sapphire.

Unfortunately, said Wilhelmina, *no. I've been tracking him for quite a while, because I'd heard rumors about a powerful mage. But I've never been able to locate him. I could locate you, Jasper, but never when you were with your father.*

"That's very strange," said Ty.

Jasper said, "He's always said that no one could ever track him. He seemed to take great pleasure in that, and sometimes when he said it, I got the idea that it was an inside joke of some kind, that he had a trick."

"Do you have any idea what that trick might be?" asked Kyle. "I've done a fair amount of tracking, usually animals, of course, and never using magic, but it's hard to deceive a good tracker. I know that Wilhelmina is one of the very best."

Jasper shook his head. "No, I've no idea. I do know that he could show up suddenly, without any warning. I wouldn't have heard him coming, and all of a sudden he'd be there. I figured he was trying to find out if I was doing what I was supposed to be doing."

Sapphire said, "That sounds like teleportation to me. Does Rastan have that ability?"

"I don't think so," said Jasper. "He does have a friend with that ability, but we haven't seen him in ages."

"What?" said Ty. "There's someone who can teleport himself?"

"Yeah," said Jasper. "My dad said that it didn't take as much strength to do that as it did to change the weather. He and his friend, Basil, would argue all the time about who was the stronger mage."

"Tell me, Jasper," said Sapphire, "could Basil transport other people or just objects?"

"People and objects," said Jasper. "He took me a couple times, and he was always taking my dad."

That would explain why I couldn't track him at times, said Wilhelmina.

"I guess that would be true," said Jasper. "I was just glad that he was somewhere else so he couldn't yell at me. Of course, now I'm somewhere else, and he still yells at me whenever he can."

"Do you know where Basil lives?" asked Ty.

"I think he lives near the palace in the capital," said Jasper. "I really don't like Basil at all. He's as self-centered as my father. He may not have ever beaten me, but he caused my father to argue and try to seem more powerful than Basil, and that was never a good thing for me."

Sapphire said, "Wilhelmina, do you think you could locate Basil?"

I'm sure going to try, said Wilhelmina. *Jasper, is Basil telepathic?*

"Oh, yes," said Jasper. "My father talks with him all the time. My father will want to brag about how much he's hurting Dragonwind and how he's going to kill all the dragons. Basil doesn't believe him, but when my father said he should come here to see for himself, Basil apparently told my father that he doesn't like cold."

Then I should be able to pick up on their telepathic communication and use that to trace Basil, said Wilhelmina.

"Excellent," said Ty. "Once you locate him, then we should be able to trace Rastan better."

"I think you should know," said Jasper, a bit hesitantly, "that both my father and Basil work for another mage, one they are both afraid of."

"What?" said Criseda. "Why didn't you mention this before?"

Jasper stuttered, "I-I-I didn't think of it until I remembered Basil."

"It's OK," said Bergamen, glaring at Criseda. "You've had a lot to deal with, and then you nearly died."

Criseda looked at the pair and then said, "Sorry, Jasper. Bergamen is right. I was just shocked that we didn't have this information, as it's pretty darned important, or so it would seem to me. Is your father doing all this for his boss?"

"No," said Jasper, "at least I don't think so. Actually, I'm not sure what either my father or Basil do for their boss, and I don't know his name either or what magical talents he may have. I just know that Basil and my father get really nervous when the boss—that's what they call him—contacts them.

I'm really sorry I don't know more. I do remember my father saying that he'd show everyone when he got rid of the dragons that he was the most powerful mage alive. I think he wanted to take his boss out but didn't have a way to do it and that his plan was intended to show his boss, as well as Basil."

Ty said, "No need to apologize, Jasper. You've given us a lot more information than we had before, and we now can look into this ourselves. We'll need to discover who all these mages are. Apparently our world has more magic than we knew, and I suspect that it's not more magic in a good way."

Martha said, "It's getting late, and these two need to get to bed. Esme, it's past your bedtime as well. I think it's time to call it a day."

Sapphire chuckled and then said, "You're quite right, Martha. Both of them are growing boys who need their rest. And Jasper is still healing. Jasper, if you remember anything else, please let Ty or Wilhelmina know."

"I will. I promise," said Jasper.

CHAPTER 14

FINDING RASTAN

Wilhelmina worked hard at trying to trace Rastan, especially whenever he was causing a snowstorm, because she knew he had to be close to Dragonwind then. Unfortunately, he seemed to have the ability to set a storm in motion and then leave it to run itself out. Since she didn't get a lot of notice about each storm, she had very little time to track Rastan. It was very frustrating.

Jasper was making progress with his telekinesis. He was a big help with snow removal in Dragonwind. In fact, the villagers kidded him and said, "Do you think you could just move the snow into the valley right outside the village?"

They were just kidding, but Jasper took up the challenge. As a result, Dragonwind was starting to look the way it normally did in winter. The men in the village were beginning to plan what to do with all the snowmelt once spring arrived.

The major change in Dragonwind involved the villagers' attitude toward Jasper and Bergamen. Even though most of them hadn't blamed Jasper for the snow, they now were seeing him as a true villager, and a major positive force at that.

The change was even more dramatic when Jasper, with some help from Bergamen in the form of an energy burst, managed at long last to push the snowstorm toward the abandoned mining towns. Jasper was exhausted, but very proud, when he got the storm to move away from Dragonwind.

Unfortunately, when Jasper did this, Wilhelmina was away from Dragonwind, trying to trace either Basil or Rastan, and so she didn't have as strong a shield around Jasper. When the cloud moved, Rastan blasted into Jasper's brain and said, *You think you can defeat me? How dare you move my storm? You are weak. You are useless. You are just a piece of scum, and your mother was very disappointed in you. Why do you think she was riding away from us when she died? She was trying to get away from you, leaving me stuck with you.*

Rastan ranted on and on. Jasper began to whimper, remembering all the abuse he'd been subjected to, but suddenly Bergamen shouted back at Rastan, *You're a miserable excuse for a human being. I've never seen such a piece of filth. Jasper is so much better off without you, and now he has real friends, not a psychopathic, murdering father!*

You dare to speak to me, you deformed, pitiful excuse for a dragon? I'll take care of you both!

Then Rastan broke off contact.

Bergamen said, "Don't you worry about him. Look how all the Dragonwind villagers love us. Look at all the good you've done for them. Winter is nearly over, and come spring, Dragonwind will be ready for the onset of your father's rains. Wilson has built more rain barrels than your father could possibly fill."

Jasper just nodded. He knew in his heart that Bergamen was right. He knew he'd made a big positive difference to Dragonwind and its villagers. Of course, what he did wouldn't have been necessary at all if it hadn't been for him. That sort of took away the pride he felt in his achievement, but it would have been much worse if he hadn't even been able to help. Then the villagers would just have been buried under all the snow, trying to clear paths and their rooftops, worrying about what would happen when all the snow melted.

Still, thought Jasper, *I have helped the morale of the village, and I have tried to fix the situation, even if it was my fault in the first place. I didn't walk away. I have made a positive difference, and isn't that what Blossom, Sapphire, Criseda, Ty, and all the others say is the point of magic? Magic should be used to help others. That's certainly not what my father believes, but I'll never be like my father.*

Esme came by then to check on Jasper. "I felt your father," she said. "Are you OK?"

"I guess," said Jasper. "Bergamen says I'm much better off without him."

"So you are," agreed Esme. "Don't you feel that?"

"Most of the time," said Jasper. "But when he starts yelling at me, I remember that he's my father and the only parent I still have and that I'm nothing but a disappointment to him."

"I'd say that's a good thing," said Esme. "I sure wouldn't want him to be proud of me, considering how evil he is."

"That's true," said Jasper.

"What do you say we all head over to the bakery and see what kind of afternoon snacks Martha has?" said Esme.

"Excellent plan," said Bergamen.

The three of them enjoyed the remainder of the afternoon. Esme was very glad for the company, because in truth she was missing Rupert and Samantha, who were helping Wilhelmina to track Rastan.

▲

Wilhelmina, Rupert, and Samantha searched the area once again for Rastan. They got lucky when Rastan started yelling telepathically at Jasper when Jasper moved the cloud. *Way to go, Jasper,* said Rupert to the others.

The three of them hurried to the place where they were sure the telepathic signal was coming from. They got there just in time to see Rastan disappear.

So he's definitely getting teleported by his friend, said Wilhelmina.

But how can we follow him now? asked Samantha.

That's where I need you two the most, said Wilhelmina. *Rupert, is the fox communication network still operating?*

Yes, answered Rupert.

Good, said Wilhelmina. *Then I need you to alert the foxes in the capital and ask them if they can sense an increase in magic anywhere near them. Just as we were able to sense Rastan's telepathic communication with Jasper, I'm hoping someone in the capital will find the telekinetic signal from Basil.*

I'll try, said Rupert. He was very still for several minutes and then said, *I've contacted two foxes in the capital and asked them to hunt.*

We may not get lucky the first time, but now that they know to look for upswings in magic, we should eventually find Basil, said Wilhelmina.

After about a half hour, Rupert said, *They say that they've found an area not too far from the palace where there seemed to be an increase in magic, but it dissipated before they could get close enough to identify the exact location.*

I'm going to contact Jasper and have him yell at his father. Tell your friends to stand by for a telepathic outburst, said Wilhelmina.

Jasper, can you contact your father and try to rile him up?

You want me to do what? asked Jasper.

I want you to make your father angry. Sorry, but to trace him we need to have him rant at you. Is Esme nearby?

She's right here with me. We're getting snacks at the bakery.

Good, said Wilhelmina. *Now let her know what you're doing. Maybe she can tag along and try to read Rastan to see what he intends now that he knows you can move his clouds. By the way, that was a great job!*

Rupert, Samantha, and Wilhelmina waited for a few minutes. While they were waiting, Rupert contacted his friends to tell them to be ready for a burst of telepathic energy.

After about ten minutes, Jasper said, *OK, we've decided I should taunt him about what he plans to do now that I can stop all his storms from hurting Dragonwind. We figure that way, we also might discover his plans. Does that sound like what you want?*

That's perfect, Jasper. Go for it, and good luck!

▲

Soon, Wilhelmina was listening to Jasper contacting his father. She not only wanted to hear the conversation, but she also wanted to be able to protect both Jasper and Esme if needed.

Jasper said, *Hey, Father! What do you plan to do now that I can stop all your storms from hitting the aerie or Dragonwind? I'll just drive them all to the abandoned mining towns, and they won't bother us at all. Some mage you are.*

Jasper's father exploded in rage. *You think you're better than me, don't you, boy? Well, I have powerful friends who will pound you into the ground. You won't stop me. You will never stop me. I will rule Dragonwind.*

So your powerful friends don't mind helping a weakling?

Weakling! I'm no weakling. I'm the only one who can do weather magic. I'm the most powerful.

Doesn't seem so powerful when I can stop it, does it? said Jasper.

But you won't be around to stop it once my friends step in. Believe me, they have real power, not just some telekinesis. You don't stand a chance.

That's not your power, though, is it? You need help. That makes you weak. You always said that the strong don't need anyone else.

At that Rastan just spluttered, and Jasper broke the connection.

Wilhelmina contacted both Jasper and Esme while Rupert checked with his friends.

You were brilliant, Jasper. Good job! And Esme, was Rastan telling the truth?

Yes, answered Esme. *At least he was telling the truth that he's got powerful friends. He wasn't too honest about his own abilities. I think even he realizes that the only reason his more powerful friends are paying attention to him is that his weather magic is a novelty. He actually seems a bit afraid of his powerful friends now that Jasper has figured out how to stop his weather meddling.*

Interesting, said Wilhelmina. *Well, thanks, and if we need you again I'll let you know, but I'm hoping Rupert's friends have located Rastan and Basil. Enjoy your snack.*

Wilhelmina turned to Rupert and said, *Any luck?*

Yes, said Rupert. *They've found the house where Rastan is staying.*

Excellent, said Wilhelmina. *Let's let Ty and Criseda know. They can get to the capital a lot faster than we can. Did you get the directions from your friends?*

Yes, and I told them to keep watch and to follow Rastan if he leaves.

Excellent, said Wilhelmina, and then she updated Ty.

Criseda and I will head out immediately, he responded. *We'll check in with Rupert's friends and keep watch. It would be nice to know who Basil and Rastan's boss is, if we can find that out.*

Thanks, said Wilhelmina. *We'll head back to Dragonwind to protect Jasper.*

CHAPTER 15

INVESTIGATIONS

Ty and Criseda flew directly to the capital and found Rupert's two friends. He checked in with them. *Hi, I'm Rupert's friend Ty, and this is Criseda. Thanks for helping us.*

I'm Harvey, said one of the foxes, *and this is Edward. We're proud to be a part of Rupert's fox communication network. I'm usually at the palace, where Rupert used to be before he moved to Dragonwind to help Esme.*

Glad to meet you both. So has anything else happened?

No, they're both still in there, said Harvey. *And no one else has come.*

You two have done a great job, Harvey. I'll be sure to let Rupert know.

So what's the plan now? asked Harvey.

I sure wish I knew what those two were talking about. Too bad we can't get inside, said Ty.

I could, said Edward, who was the smallest fox Ty had ever seen.

Ty looked at him and said, *You could?*

Sure, said Edward, who then turned and ran for the back of the house.

Harvey said, *He got really tired of always being called "runt," so he decided to find a way to make his size an advantage. He's become a master at breaking into places and not getting caught.*

They all waited, and sure enough, Edward soon called to them, *I'm in. There are two men here, and they're arguing. I'll listen and then let you know what's going on.*

Harvey turned to Ty and Criseda and said, *We don't call him runt anymore.*

I certainly couldn't have done that, said Criseda, and the fox chuckled.

Then they all settled in to wait for Edward. Finally, after a little more than an hour, Edward reappeared. He said, *There's just the one guy there now, the one named Basil. Rastan has gone back to Dragonwind. Basil sent him there. Both of them are scared of a third guy that they just called "the boss." From what I heard, the boss only cares about them because of their magic. Basil is still useful because he can teleport the boss when needed. But now that Jasper has conquered his father's weather magic, Rastan is scared the boss doesn't have any use for him, and apparently the boss tends to kill off those who are no longer useful. Rastan has gone back to Dragonwind to try to find a way to defeat or eliminate Jasper.*

You learned a lot, said Ty. *Thank you!*

I'm sorry I couldn't find out who their boss is, said Edward.

It's always possible that Rastan and Basil don't know his real name. But you found out a lot, and Criseda and I need to get to Dragonwind right away to protect Jasper. It sounds as if Rastan is going to try to capture or kill him so that he can save his own skin. We wouldn't have known that without you, Edward. We also wouldn't have known that Rastan has gone. So, many thanks.

Edward gave a little bow, and Harvey said, *We'll continue to watch here, and we can let Rupert know if Basil leaves or does anything or if anyone visits him.*

That would be really helpful, Harvey. Thanks! said Ty, and he vaulted onto Criseda.

⋏

On the way back to Dragonwind, Ty contacted Wilhelmina. *Rastan has returned to Dragonwind, and he's determined to capture or kill Jasper.*

We'll keep him safe, said Wilhelmina. *See you soon.*

⋏

When Ty and Criseda arrived in Dragonwind, they went immediately to Martha's to talk with Jasper, Bergamen, Esme, Rupert, Samantha, and Wilhelmina.

"First of all, Jasper, that was incredibly brave of you to confront your father," said Ty.

"I think it was a good thing," said Jasper. "I was really scared when I started, but all of a sudden, I realized that I have the power to stop him. He's not the all-powerful mage I always thought he was. I'm not saying that if I met him face-to-face I wouldn't panic, but I'm beginning to see him as vulnerable."

"That's a huge change, Jasper," said Criseda.

"Now, we need to let you know what Rupert's friend Harvey discovered," said Ty.

"It was really Edward who learned the most," corrected Criseda.

What? That little runt? said Rupert.

"I suggest," said Ty, "that you don't call him 'runt' anymore. He's now capitalizing on his small size, and he actually went into Basil's house all by himself and listened to their conversation."

What? exclaimed Rupert.

"Precisely," said Criseda. "No one else wanted to try to get inside. In fact, we thought Edward was being reckless. But he got us the best information."

Ty went on to explain all that they had learned. When he was finished, Jasper said, "So my father needs either to capture or kill me in order to stay alive. This isn't just that he hates me and doesn't want anyone alive who's stronger than him. This is his life at stake now."

"I'm afraid so," said Ty. "But we aren't going to let him get anywhere near you."

"We want to capture him, right?" said Jasper. "So why don't we let him try to capture me?"

"You want to be the bait in a trap?" said Esme. "That could go wrong in so many ways."

"But you'd all be there guarding me," said Jasper.

Ty said, "We really appreciate your faith in us, but you do realize that Basil could teleport you in a flash, and we couldn't stop him?"

"True," said Jasper, "but you know where he lives. If my father did that, you and Criseda, for instance, could be waiting at Basil's and grab us all. Or better still, as soon as my father has me, you grab Basil, and nobody goes anywhere."

"OK," said Esme, "but your father doesn't seem to want you alive. What if he just knifes you or shoots you with an arrow? We couldn't stop that."

"I could stop the arrow with my telekinesis," said Jasper.

"If you saw it coming," said Criseda. "There are just too many things that could go wrong."

Bergamen said, "I nearly lost you once. I can't lose you again. If you're going, then so am I."

"Bergamen, no. We need my father to get to his boss," said Jasper, "and I'm the one he wants. He doesn't want you at all, and he's more likely to kill you outright."

Ty listened to all the arguments and then said, "I think we might stand a chance of doing this successfully if we plan really well. Esme, you will be crucial to our success, because we need to have you read Rastan's intent, what he's planning to do."

"But what if I'm wrong?" she said.

"I've never known you to be wrong," Ty answered. "It's possible that Rastan will try this all on his own, without Basil. We'll need to know what his plans are."

"But we don't know where Rastan is," said Esme. "How am I supposed to read his intentions if I don't know where he is?"

"I think we do know where he is," said Ty. "Wilhelmina, where was Rastan when he teleported to the capital?"

He was just outside Dragonwind, in front of a cave on the east side.

"Good," said Ty. "That's where we start. Chances are he'll be there at least long enough to pack. We'll need to go now and check it out. If he is there, then Esme, you can read his intentions, and we'll know how to plan."

Everyone stood up, but Esme said, "I still don't like this."

"Neither do I," said Bergamen.

"Let's give it a try," said Ty. "It's getting too late to do the entire plan, but let's see if Esme, Rupert, Samantha, and I can see what he's up to."

With that Ty and the other three moved out of the village, heading east. Ty sent Rupert and Samantha ahead to scout. Rupert called back, *You were right, Ty. He's here, packing his things into a large sack.*

"OK, Esme," said Ty. "Carefully sneak a bit closer and see if you can get a read on him."

Esme got down on her hands and knees and crawled forward. She found a large boulder to hide behind, and then she tried to read Rastan. At first she couldn't discern anything, but then she realized it was because she was so nervous and was trying too hard. She relaxed, and soon she was in Rastan's mind. She saw that he really wanted to kill Jasper. But she also saw that he figured he'd have more clout with the boss if he captured Jasper and took him in. He figured the boss would be thrilled to have Jasper. He was going to shift his location to another nearby cave, and then he was going to cause a major earthquake first thing in the morning, when he was strongest. The earthquake would damage most of Dragonwind. He was going to open up the major crevasse that ran underneath the village. As everyone was running around in a panic, Rastan would walk into the village and snatch Jasper. Then he'd call Basil to teleport them both to Basil's house.

Esme realized that Rastan didn't want to call Basil until he actually had Jasper, because he didn't want to look a fool if his plan didn't work. Esme slowly crawled back to Ty. Ty asked Rupert and Samantha to stand guard and follow Rastan if he left. Then Ty and Esme went silently back to the village hall to meet with the others.

"Well?" asked Ty.

"You guessed right," said Esme. "He really wants Jasper dead, but he figures that his boss will be impressed if Rastan gives him Jasper, so that's what he's planning to do." Esme went on to explain about the earthquake and the snatch and finally about him calling Basil to teleport them.

"So it's as I thought," said Ty. "But we'll have to force his hand before he does an earthquake. We don't want the village damaged and people hurt or killed. Jasper, are you really determined to do this?"

"Yes," said Jasper.

"OK, then," said Ty. "Here's what we're going to do." Ty explained his plan as they had dinner, and they all discussed it, trying to find flaws, tweaking the weak spots, trying to foresee every eventuality, until finally they had the best plan they could come up with. Everyone then headed to bed. They knew they needed to be well rested, and they wanted to be at Rastan's cave before the sun rose.

Early the next morning, when it was still dark outside, Rupert and Samantha explained exactly where Rastan's new cave was, having tracked him there. Ty, Jasper, and Bergamen rode on Criseda until they were near Rastan's new location. Jasper was determined to walk into his father's cave alone, but Bergamen knew that Rastan would never believe that Jasper wasn't trying to trap him.

"He knows you'd never leave me. If you come without me," said Bergamen, "your father will know it's a trap."

Ty said, "He's got a point."

"But..." said Jasper.

"No buts," said Bergamen. "We go together or not at all."

"Jasper, I hate to admit it, but I think Bergamen has a valid point. We don't want your father to guess what we're up to."

CHAPTER 16

CAPTURE

Jasper and Bergamen walked toward Rastan's cave. They stopped out in front and Jasper called, "Father, could we talk with you?"

"You want to talk with me?" said Rastan as he stepped out of the cave. "Why?"

"I hoped that now that you see that your storms won't affect Dragonwind, you might be willing just to leave us alone and go somewhere else."

"Is that what you think? You think you've defeated me? Well, I have news for you. I'm more powerful than you think," said Rastan.

"Only because you have another mage helping you," said Jasper, who really wanted to taunt his father.

"Well, you aren't as smart as you think you are," said Rastan as he stepped closer to Jasper and Bergamen.

Suddenly, Rastan grabbed Jasper's left arm and then kicked viciously at Bergamen as he shouted, "Now."

Rastan and Jasper both disappeared just as Ty and Criseda charged into the clearing in front of the cave. Bergamen was huddled next to a rock, sobbing, "I couldn't stop him. I couldn't protect Jasper."

Ty ran over to Bergamen and saw that his front right leg was broken from the kick. Ty tried to comfort the poor dragon. "There was no way you could stop Rastan, and we knew this could happen. We're prepared for this.

Let me get you back to Martha, and I'll ask Blossom to come help with your leg. Criseda and I are flying directly to Basil's place, and I'll also let Harvey know."

With that, Ty gently picked up Bergamen, jumped onto Criseda, and flew to Dragonwind. On the short flight, he contacted Esme. *Warn Martha that Bergamen's coming, and he's injured—broken right leg. Call Blossom for me, please. We're just going to drop Bergamen in Dragonwind and then fly to Basil's, where Jasper should be.*

OK, I'll do that and wait for you on the village green, said Esme.

Ty landed very briefly, just long enough to hand Bergamen to Kyle, who'd come out with Esme. As he took off, he said, *Let Rupert know what's going on. I'll contact Harvey.*

Esme nodded and followed Kyle inside as Bergamen cried out, *Find him, Ty! Please.*

Ty called back, *I will, and I'll let you know what we find.*

With that, Ty and Criseda disappeared from sight. As they were flying, Ty tried first to contact Jasper, but he had no luck. Then he contacted Harvey. *Did Rastan and Jasper just arrive at Basil's?*

Yes, said Harvey, *and now Rastan and Basil are questioning him. Edward has gone inside, and he's reporting back to us.*

Keep me posted, said Ty. *We'll be with you as quickly as we can.*

Harvey updated Ty every ten minutes or so while they were on their flight. Rastan was whipping Jasper to get him to answer questions about the dragons, about his magic, about who was helping him, and so forth, but Jasper refused to open his mouth. Rastan grew angrier and angrier. His blows grew increasingly intense and vicious. Finally Jasper collapsed into unconsciousness.

Ty heard Bergamen whimpering as he said, *Jasper's in a lot of pain. I can feel that.*

Ty and Criseda arrived right after that. "Want me to tear that house apart and get Jasper?" asked Criseda.

Ty chuckled, in spite of the seriousness of the situation, and said, "No, let's get the latest from Harvey."

Edward's reporting that Rastan and Basil are arguing about what to do next and whether they should take Jasper to the boss. If they don't do that, then they plan just to kill Jasper.

That's not good either way, said Ty. *Maybe we should rescue Jasper now.*

We don't know anything more than we did before Jasper was captured. He wants us to get more information. We have to give him a chance.

Just then Edward shouted, *They've teleported again. They said they were going to the boss's house, but they didn't say where that was!*

Can you track where they went? asked Ty.

Maybe, said Harvey as he sniffed into the air. Edward came out of the house and helped. Eventually, Harvey said, *This way,* and the two of them headed out to the south, away from the palace and the center of town.

Ty and Criseda flew above Harvey and Edward. They knew they didn't have the ability to track Jasper, but they kept watch on the foxes while also looking for anything that might be a sign from Jasper.

Ty said, "I still can't reach Jasper telepathically. I hope that's only because Rastan and Basil are blocking us."

"That does seem the most likely reason," said Criseda. "They don't seem ready to kill him just yet."

"Harvey and Edward do still seem to be following some trail," said Ty.

"Hope it's the right one and that it doesn't disappear," said Criseda.

"I know I promised to keep Bergamen informed, but I don't think it would be helpful to let him know we've lost Jasper," said Ty.

"Yeah, let's wait a bit. Maybe Harvey will find him before we have to let Bergamen know," agreed Criseda.

The two of them circled overhead, keeping themselves centered over Harvey. The foxes were moving confidently, so Ty crossed his fingers and hoped that they'd locate Jasper, and with him this mysterious boss.

Finally, after about an hour, Harvey stopped. He looked up at Criseda and then said, *We were really close, but now we've lost them.*

What does that mean? asked Ty.

Well, the signal just stopped. It didn't fade out, as it will with time. Instead it just ceased, as if they were no longer teleporting. They've gone somewhere in this area on foot, but we can't find a trail to follow.

We're going to land, said Ty, *and then I'll help while Criseda flies above us. Jasper might be able to give us a sign.*

Criseda landed long enough for Ty to jump off and then took off again. This was a poorer area of the capital, and the residents weren't used to seeing dragons.

Ty looked around him and then went into a small apothecary shop. The proprietor hurried over to see if he could be of any assistance. "How can I help you, sir? Are you lost?"

"No," said Ty. "But I'm wondering if there's a home nearby that belongs to someone powerful. I heard this area was governed by a person in authority."

"I don't know if I'd call him a person in authority," said the proprietor. "At least he certainly shouldn't be. But it is true that an evil man named Claude lives close by. He's a money lender who charges exorbitantly high interest rates, and he controls most of the lives in this part of the capital."

"That could be who I'm looking for," said Ty. "What can you tell me about him?"

"He grew up here on the streets. But he hasn't stayed here, really. You remember the problems we had, with child slavery and the like?"

Ty nodded, and the proprietor hesitated but then continued. "Well, King Bertram stripped at least four nobles of their estates as a result, and he's opened up all those lands for those who want to make a decent life for themselves. That's a really good thing, but Claude and probably some others are ruining it. He's been tricking—stealing, really—properties from the new owners and renters. He's looking to get most of those old estates. It's not right what he's doing, but no one seems to know that he's doing it. I wish someone would tell King Bertram, because I think the king's a good man, and he wouldn't like this."

Ty said, "Trust me, he wouldn't, and I'll be sure to tell him. I'm a roving ambassador for the king, and I can act on his behalf. Meanwhile, I think a friend of mine might have been brought to Claude. Can you tell me where he lives?"

"He's in the big brick house at the end of this street. And good luck to you, sir. Our neighborhood really needs help. I'm not afraid of Claude. I've had a good life and I'm not under his control, but I'm about the only one who can say that."

Ty went back outside as Criseda landed. He then spoke to Criseda, Harvey, and the others. "Apparently there is someone named Claude who lives in the brick house at the end of the street. He's someone I need to check out for sure, even if he doesn't have Jasper, but he also might be the so-called boss that Rastan and Basil were talking about. Any ideas?"

Yes, said Edward. *Let me scout around first. Wait here.* And off Edward ran.

Well, I guess he told us, said Harvey. *But he's right. He's the one most likely to get inside and get us information. So I guess we wait.*

Ty turned to Criseda and said, "We've got lots of folks staring at us."

"You mean staring at me," she answered.

As she said that, a young girl about six years old with long blond pigtails and blue eyes came up to them and then said shyly, "Are you a good dragon?"

Criseda bowed her head and said, "Yes, I am. My name is Criseda. What's yours?"

"I'm Jennie. You sure are pretty."

A woman about thirty years old, also with long blond hair, which she wore in a ponytail, and blue eyes approached from the end of the street. "Jennie, come here. Don't bother those folks."

Ty smiled and said, "She's not bothering us at all. Is she your daughter?"

The woman was hesitant to get any closer, so Ty walked over to her. He held out his hand and said, "I'm Ty. I'm an ambassador for King Bertram. What's your name?"

"You know King Bertram?" the woman said. "Is he a good man?"

"Yes, he's a very good man, and he tries hard to be a good king as well," said Ty.

The woman thought for several minutes. She looked around to see if anyone was close enough to overhear them. Finally, she said very softly, "My name is Irene, and yes, Jennie is my daughter. We live over there." She waved her hand vaguely down the street. "This isn't a very good neighborhood. A man named Claude lives here. He should know better. He grew up here, but he figured out how to lend money to folks and then charge them a lot of interest. He's gotten really rich, but there are a lot of people here who can't afford to make their payments. He hurts them. Sometimes they end up dead. He's got folks working for him as can do magic. I don't think that's right, either, but maybe you think differently."

Ty looked at the woman and said, "Magic itself is neither good nor bad. It just is. But how it's used is important. I can do some magic, and so can my dragon, Criseda. However, we only ever use it to help others. We would never use it to harm anyone, although we have used it to catch others who are causing harm."

"Truly?" asked Irene.

"Definitely," said Ty. "I just learned about Claude, and I can tell you that the king will hear about him, and he won't be allowed to continue to hurt people or steal from them. My friends and I"—Ty turned to wave to Harvey and Criseda—"are here to try to find a friend of ours, a young boy, whom we think Claude has in his house."

Irene looked at Ty carefully, weighing his words. Then she looked at Jennie, who by now was chatting happily with Criseda. Criseda had bent her left foreleg, and Jennie was sitting on it. Finally, Irene nodded to herself, as if she'd reached a decision, and she said, "Then you should know, there are rumors about that house. Some say that there are tunnels below it that cross back and forth under this part of the city. I don't know if that's true, but certainly Claude has ways of coming and going that no one sees. Be careful. He's powerful."

Ty said, "Thank you for the information. Do you know if Claude can do magic?"

Irene laughed. "No, not him. I've heard him say that all magic is just a sham but that he's happy to make use of those who think they're better than the rest of us. I don't think he can do anything like that, but I do know that he's able to make people do things that they don't want to do because he knows stuff about them or because they owe him money."

Irene was quiet for a few minutes, and then she said, "We learned that the hard way. Claude convinced my husband that he could make a lot of money if he went into some scheme with him. Of course we didn't have the money for that, but Claude said he'd be happy to loan it. Before we knew it, my husband owed much more than he'd borrowed. He got so deeply into debt that there was no hope that he'd ever get free. There are lots of folks around here like that. But my husband was a good man, and he couldn't handle the pressure from Claude. He ended up killing himself. Now it's just Jennie and me. Claude comes by every now and again and tells us that he hasn't forgotten what my husband owed him. Then he looks at Jennie, and not in a good way, if you get my meaning. She's only six now, but you can already see that she's going to be really pretty. I don't know what's to become of us now."

Ty was horrified by Irene's story. Finally he asked, "Do you have family and friends here in the capital?"

"No," said Irene. "We came here when we heard that there were more opportunities, especially when all the new lands opened up. But we never got any."

"Would you be able to move if I could take you somewhere much nicer, where the two of you would be safe?"

"In a heartbeat," Irene said, "but we don't have any money to start over."

"Listen," said Ty. "I have to see about rescuing a young friend, so I can't do anything now."

"That's OK," said Irene.

"No," said Ty. "That's not what I meant. We aren't far from the palace. Could you and Jennie get there?"

As he asked, he pulled a piece of parchment out of his jacket and wrote a note.

Irene said hesitantly, "I guess so."

"OK, then this is what you must do, because I don't know what's going to happen here, and we'll probably be making Claude very mad. I don't want you to get hurt. You pack up your belongings. Don't tell anyone where you are going. Head to the palace, and when you get there, give this note to the guard on the gate and tell him that Ty and Criseda said that you are to be kept safe until he can come get you and take you to Dragonwind. Can you remember all that?"

Irene took the piece of paper and tucked it safely into her skirt pocket, and then she looked Ty straight in the face and repeated, "Give this to the guard on the palace gate and tell him that we're to wait for Ty and Criseda, and he's to keep us safe until you can take us to Dragonwind."

"That's right," said Ty. "And remember, don't tell anyone else."

"Thank you, sir," said Irene.

Ty smiled and said, "Just call me Ty. Everyone else does."

Irene nodded and then called to Jennie, "Time we were getting home now."

The two of them left back down the street, and Ty couldn't help noticing that the woman walked with more confidence than before. He sure hoped she'd make it to the palace. He decided to contact King Bertram telepathically.

Bertram, I'm in the capital, in the poor section. I've learned some very disquieting things about a man here named Claude. I'll share all that with you later. But I want you to alert your guards. I'm hoping that a woman named Irene and her six-year-old daughter Jennie will be showing up at the palace gate with a note from me. They're in a horrific situation, and I want to get them out to Dragonwind. Can you have someone look after them until Criseda and I can get to you?

Rescuing more folks in need, huh? the king replied. Ty could almost hear the chuckle in Bertram's thoughts. *Of course, and stay safe yourself.*

Thanks, Sire!

Ty was explaining to Criseda what he'd done when Edward returned to report. *Jasper is there,* Edward began, *but it's not going to be easy to get him out. This Claude guy is the one in charge. He has a bunch of thugs guarding the house. Both Rastan and Basil are also there. Claude seems to be upset with them. But the worst part is that this house has a real maze of tunnels underneath it. I nearly got trapped in one. Thugs are coming and going all the time. I did manage to find the room where Jasper is now, and I let him see me. I figured the kid needed some good news. I watched Rastan whip him again because he wouldn't answer questions. We really do need to get him out of there. I just don't know how.*

Ty said, "Thanks, Edward. I met someone who told me that there were rumors of a maze of tunnels, but I was hoping it wasn't true."

It's true, all right. I saw them. And they're keeping Jasper in the basement, with Basil and Rastan watching him.

Criseda said, "We need more help, and we need more information. How are we going to get that?"

CHAPTER 17

NEW ARRIVALS

Ty, where are you? We're here to help, said Wilhelmina.

Ty explained their location, and in a few minutes Wilhelmina, with Esme, Rupert, and Samantha, walked down the street, to the amazement of the inhabitants of the area.

Ty smiled when he saw them. He said, "What brings you four here? Not that we aren't happy to see you."

Esme said, "Bergamen was not happy at being left behind, but with the cast on his leg, even he had to admit he'd be more of a hindrance than a help. He's also suffering badly from Jasper's whippings, crying in pain with each blow. However, he was frantic that we get here as quickly as we could. He kept saying that his mother had foreseen something like this and that you'd need us for some maze. So we left about three hours ago and came as quickly as we could. Does that make any sense to you?"

"Actually, it does," said Criseda. "We know where Jasper is, but we can't get to him. He's in the basement of that brick house at the end of the street, but the house is sitting on a large maze of tunnels that crisscross underneath this entire area. There are various access points, which we don't know, and Claude, who's apparently Rastan and Basil's boss, has lots of henchmen who come and go through the tunnels. We have no idea how many of them are inside."

I've been inside, said Edward, *and I did manage to get a glimpse of Jasper, so he knows that someone is here looking for him, but he can't do much.*

So, if I understand this, said Wilhelmina, *you need to know how many men Claude has down there and where the tunnel access points are so that you can figure out how to get to Jasper quickly, before Basil can teleport him again. Well, that doesn't sound too hard, does it, guys?*

No, we've got it, said Rupert as Samantha nodded in agreement.

Esme added, "This is why Bergamen said we were needed, but I don't understand how Windsong knew this months ago."

Criseda said, "Windsong had the gift of prophecy. It's a very rare gift, and honestly, it's not one that dragons, at least as long as we're living isolated in the aerie, need. I think that's one of the main reasons Windsong left. I think she wanted to be able to use her gift to help others. We can be very grateful that she did and that she shared as much as she could with Bergamen."

Ty nodded in agreement and then said, "So how do you four plan to help? You seem to have more ideas than we do."

Esme smiled and said, "That's because of my magic. I will be able to walk along the streets and sense the intentions of anyone around me, including those who might be *under* me."

Ty laughed. "That's brilliant!"

We're also planning on having Samantha help Edward. If they can sneak inside again, then they can help us track the fastest route to Jasper, said Rupert. *Harvey and I should be able to keep in communication with the two of them and then pass the information on to one of you.*

Once everyone is in position, said Wilhelmina, *Criseda and I can do a lot of stomping up here, over tunnels we find that you don't need. Hopefully, we'll not only be a distraction, but we also might cause some of those tunnels to collapse. But we need to wait to do that until you actually have Jasper so that Basil doesn't panic and teleport him somewhere else.*

"Sounds as if we have a plan," said Ty. "You're up first, Esme. Edward, can you show Samantha how you got into Claude's house?"

It's easy, said Edward. *Come on, and I'll show you.*

As Edward and Samantha ran off, Rupert and Harvey moved down the street to be closer to the house, staying out of sight.

While they were waiting, Ty told Wilhelmina about what they'd learned from Irene and Jennie. "I've been noticing that this neighborhood doesn't seem vibrant or alive, as you'd expect. We don't see many people, and those we do see look fearful."

"That could be due to the presence of a dragon and a large moose," said Criseda.

"True, but I don't think so," said Ty. "When people look at you, I see more smiles than anything else. Jennie certainly didn't seem unduly afraid of you. She was cautious, but that's only sensible."

Rupert broke into their conversation. *I just heard from Edward, and he and Samantha are inside Claude's house. Jasper is still in the basement, and Rastan and Basil are also in the basement with him. Edward is going to explore for tunnel entrances while Samantha stays near Jasper. She's hoping to get to talk with him, or at least let him know that she's there.*

Thanks, Rupert, said Wilhelmina. Keep us posted on any changes.

Ty, said Esme. *There are a lot of people in the tunnels. I'm picking up at least a dozen separate minds. There seems to be a network of small tunnels leading to a central tunnel that enters the house. The men are in small groups of two or three, as far as I can tell.*

Have you identified Claude?

Not yet. I hear about him from his men, and he's certainly not popular. Everyone seems afraid of him. I'm going to move closer to the house.

Be careful, said Ty. *If Rastan and Basil are afraid of him even though he might not actually have any magic of his own, then he must be a major threat.*

I will be careful. But we need to know what his intentions are.

Ty, said Rupert, *tell Esme that Edward just told me that Claude is going downstairs to talk with Basil and Rastan. He also says that there's a basement window on the south side of the house. That's how they got in, and it's partly open, so Esme might be able to hear Claude.*

Thanks, Rupert, said Ty before he quickly switched back to Esme and told her the news.

I'm on my way, said Esme.

Ty then passed on all the news to Wilhelmina and Criseda before saying, "It's nerve-wracking to have them all in danger while we just hang around."

"I agree," said Criseda. "But we can't exactly be inconspicuous. Edward might not like getting teased about his size, but there are times when it's a real advantage."

Tell me about it, said Wilhelmina. *I have no memory of ever being small.*

The three of them had no choice but to wait. They were about to simply storm into Claude's house when they saw Esme running toward them.

"Help!" she called. "Claude is going to kill Jasper!"

Ty jumped onto Criseda's back and reached down for Esme to pull her up. "Let's go," said Ty, and Criseda took flight, heading for Claude's home. Wilhelmina was right behind them, thundering along the road. As they approached the house, Esme said, "I think Claude also plans to kill Rastan and Basil, since they can't help him now that Jasper's power has grown, but I honestly don't care about that."

It didn't take long to reach the home, and Criseda began pulling the roof off. She was going to rip the house apart, floor by floor.

Rupert called to them, *Edward and Samantha are with Jasper. Samantha has chewed his ropes and nearly has him free. Rastan and Boris have teleported out of there, leaving Jasper to Claude, who is on his way down to the basement. Harvey and I are at the basement window, but it's not big enough to get Jasper out that way.*

Ty said, "Hang on. We're coming. Did you hear that, Wilhelmina? The south basement window."

On my way.

Criseda swooped down from the torn roof and landed in the backyard. Ty and Esme jumped down and ran to the basement window. Criseda joined them, and without any hesitation, she hooked her claws around the window frame and pulled the entire window out of the wall.

Esme was the smallest, so she ran to the opening and crawled in. Rupert, Samantha, and Jasper were all there. Samantha had just freed Jasper, who looked dazed and confused. Esme went over to Jasper and said, "Here, Jasper, let me help you. And everyone else, get out of here."

Jasper said, "Where am I?"

Ty was at the window, pulling at bricks to make the opening wider. He said, "We'll tell you everything later. Just get over here, now."

Esme bent down and picked up a flask and then helped Jasper move to the window. Ty grabbed him and lifted him out of the opening. Jasper screamed as Ty lifted him, but Ty was more concerned with getting him out than minding his wounds. Esme, Edward, and Samantha followed quickly. By then Harvey and Rupert had joined in the rescue efforts. Ty told Rupert, Samantha, Edward, and Esme to get onto Wilhelmina while he and Criseda took Jasper and Harvey.

"To the palace," said Ty as Criseda took off.

Wilhelmina thundered out of the yard just as Claude came around the corner of the house. Esme saw that he had a bow and arrow, and she told Wilhelmina to run faster. Claude got a shot off, but he missed. His arrow grazed Wilhelmina's left flank but didn't do much damage. It certainly didn't slow her down at all. She rounded the corner into the street and just kept right on running.

Ty, Criseda, Jasper, and Harvey were the first to arrive at the palace. Criseda landed in the palace courtyard, and Ty jumped down. He helped Harvey and then carefully lifted Jasper down.

"I don't feel good," said Jasper. "My back hurts." He then collapsed into unconsciousness.

"Don't worry," said Ty. "We'll get you help now. You're safe."

But Jasper didn't hear him.

A palace guard came running up to Ty, and Ty said, "Wilhelmina will be arriving any minute. Please let her and her passengers in as soon as they get here."

"Yes, sir," said the guard as he saluted and went back to the gate.

Ty carried Jasper to the front door of the palace. He was about to knock when Henry opened the door. "Bring the young man into the sitting room," he said.

"Thanks, Henry," answered Ty. "He needs a doctor."

"The palace doctor is on his way," said Henry. "Criseda alerted the king to your needs."

"Oh, Henry, this is Harvey," said Ty. "He's been helping with the rescue."

"Yes, sir," said Henry. "I know Harvey quite well. He brings messages for King Bertram from time to time."

"Wilhelmina, Esme, Rupert, Edward, and Samantha should be here any minute," said Ty.

"I'll be sure to welcome them all," said Henry.

King Bertram entered the sitting room then and said, "What's wrong with this young man?"

"Sire, this is Jasper. He and Bergamen, his dragon, are living in Dragonwind, but Jasper was kidnapped, and now I honestly don't know what's wrong with him. His back is bleeding, but that doesn't explain his disorientation before he passed out. I told you about his father, Rastan, when I was here last. Well, Rastan kidnapped him with the help of another mage named Basil, who can teleport. We found them in the poor section of the capital, in the house of a man named Claude. But now I don't know what's wrong with Jasper."

"I may know," said Esme as she hurried into the room.

"Hi, Esme," said King Bertram, and she nodded to him but went right over to Jasper.

"Rastan figured out that Claude was probably going to kill Basil and Rastan and flee the capital. He told Basil, and Basil said they had to get out of there fast. Rastan wanted to take Jasper, but Basil refused. He said he'd had enough of the brat—his words, not mine. Rastan said that they couldn't leave Jasper to talk to Claude, so Rastan pulled a flask out of his jacket and forced Jasper to drink and said, as he dropped the flask to the floor, 'That'll take care of him. We won't see him again.' With that, Rastan and Basil disappeared."

"Poisoned," said Ty. "But what poison?"

Doctor Brunfeld walked in just then, saying, "Did you say poison? Let me have a look at the young man."

Esme looked at the white-haired, stooped-shouldered elderly man with the doctor's bag. He had very kind eyes, and Esme just hoped he really knew a lot. She held out a flask and said, "I took this after the men left. This flask held the poison, but there doesn't seem to be much left. Will it help you?"

Dr. Brunfeld looked at Esme and said, "Brilliant, young lady. This will hopefully help a lot. Now, tell me about his symptoms."

Ty answered this time. "When we broke into the room where Jasper was being held, I noticed that Jasper seemed really confused. Yet we'd heard him fighting off his father's interrogations earlier, so that made no sense to me. He screamed when I picked him up to get him through the window. As we arrived here, he said he didn't feel good and his back hurt. Then he collapsed into unconsciousness."

Dr. Brunfeld shouted out the door, "Roland, here, now!"

A tall young man with short brown hair and brown eyes bustled into the room, saying, "Yes, Dr. Brunfeld?"

"I need to know what was in this flask, and I need to know *now*," Dr. Brunfeld said as he handed the flask to Roland.

"Right away, sir."

Roland started to leave, and Dr. Brunfeld said, "Be careful. It's a powerful, fast-acting poison that causes disorientation followed by unconsciousness. That should give you some ideas about what to start testing for."

"Yes, sir." And Roland hurried away.

Esme said, "You will be able to save him, won't you?"

"I'll certainly do my very best," said Dr. Brunfeld as he bent to examine Jasper. When he turned Jasper over, all of them gasped. Jasper's back was shredded and bleeding from being whipped. Finally, the doctor stood up and said, "He's been given a very powerful poison. And he's not in the best shape. I can see that he's been tortured recently."

Criseda stuck her head in the doorway and said, "I've just contacted Blossom and Bergamen. Blossom has just left Dragonwind with both Martha and Bergamen, and she's going to fly as fast as she can. She should be here in less than an hour."

Ty said, "Thanks, Criseda." He was now kneeling by Jasper and using his healing magic. He hoped he'd be able to strengthen Jasper's resistance and, if nothing else, slow down the poison until an antidote could be found. At the very least, he could try to heal Jasper's back.

King Bertram began shifting some of the furniture to the side of the room as he said, "Please come in, Criseda. And, yes, thank you."

Dr. Brunfeld said, "Who are these folks that Criseda mentioned?"

"Blossom is the dragon with the most healing powers," said King Bertram. "Martha is a fantastic herbalist and healer who raised Ty and is now raising Esme. And Bergamen is the dragon whom Jasper is bonded to."

"Ah, I see," said Dr. Brunfeld. "Well, they will all be most welcome additions to our consultations. This young man is going to need all the help we can give him. Who was the devil who poisoned him?"

"His father," said Esme with disgust in her voice. "He's also the one who whipped him."

Roland came hurrying back into the room, carrying a vial. He said, "I've analyzed the poison, and it's a very rare one, based on a variant of henbane. I've mixed an antidote. It did neutralize the poison in the lab. I can only hope it will do the same for this young man."

"Jasper," said Esme. "His name is Jasper."

"Yes," said Roland. "I hope this works for Jasper."

Dr. Brunfeld took the vial from Roland, smelled it, took a drop on his tongue, and then nodded to his assistant. "Excellent job."

Then Dr. Brunfeld went to Jasper and had Ty lift his head up so that the antidote could be dripped into Jasper's mouth. At first it just dribbled out again. Jasper wasn't swallowing. Dr. Brunfeld stroked Jasper's throat and then tried again. Eventually he managed to get Jasper to swallow.

"Now we'll just have to wait and see if this helps him."

The group was silent, each member lost in their own thoughts, but Ty could hear Bergamen telepathically. *I hurt, my back hurts, my mind is cloudy, what's happening to me?*

Ty realized that Bergamen was feeling what Jasper was suffering. Ty tried to calm Bergamen.

CHAPTER 18

WAITING

Queen Elicia, a tall, slender woman in her thirties with red hair and blue eyes, walked into the room, followed by Irene. Elicia said, "So you found him, Ty."

"Yes, we did, but not before he was badly whipped and then poisoned. He's now fighting for his life," said Ty, who also nodded to Irene, glad that she'd made it to the palace.

Just then Blossom arrived, along with Martha and Bergamen. Ty said, "Let me introduce these new arrivals. Blossom is the dragons' healer, Martha is a renowned herbalist and healer from Dragonwind, and Bergamen is Jasper's partner."

Martha blushed at the introduction, but Queen Elicia went right over to her and said, "I'm so glad to meet you after all these years. I've heard so much about you from Ty and Esme."

Martha began to curtsy, but Queen Elicia gave her a big hug instead. Then she introduced Martha to Irene, who looked relieved to see someone who seemed to be closer to her social station.

Bergamen hobbled over to Jasper and sat as close to him as he could. "What's wrong with him?" Bergamen asked.

Dr. Brunfeld went over to the young dragon and said gently, "He's been poisoned, and he's also been badly whipped."

"I knew we shouldn't have let him near his father. It was Jasper's plan, but I just knew," wailed Bergamen.

Dr. Brunfeld said, "It looks as if you've been in a battle yourself."

"It's nothing," said Bergamen. "Nothing like what Jasper's got."

Blossom and Martha both moved over to the couch, where Jasper was lying unconscious. Blossom said, "Do you know what the poison is?"

Dr. Brunfeld said, "We've found an antidote, but we don't know if it's strong enough or in fact if Jasper is strong enough to fight the poison even with the antidote's help."

Blossom and Martha both nodded with understanding. Blossom said, "So we just have to wait."

"Unfortunately, yes," said Dr. Brunfeld.

"Isn't there anything we can do?" asked Bergamen.

Ty bent over Jasper. Already Jasper's back looked better after his healing efforts, but Ty realized that it wouldn't matter if the back got healed if Jasper succumbed to the poison. His healing efforts needed to go toward blocking the poison. He looked up at Martha and said, "Do you by any chance have your healing salve, the one you used on me when I was whipped?"

Martha looked into her healer's bag and pulled out a jar. "You mean this?"

Ty smiled. "I should have known. Let's turn Jasper onto his side so you can put it on his back."

Dr. Brunfeld watched as Martha worked. They talked about ingredients and what they'd found to be most effective on various wounds.

Blossom looked at Bergamen's leg and then said to Ty, "I think your healing magic could heal this break if you feel up to it."

"I know," said Ty. "I didn't want to take time before Criseda and I left Dragonwind, because Jasper was in danger."

"I don't care about my leg," said Bergamen. "You're right to put Jasper first."

Ty smiled at the little dragon, who now was not so little. Then he said, "I've done all that I can for Jasper. Please, let me see if I can help you. Jasper would want that, I know."

"OK," said Bergamen, a little reluctantly. "If you're sure Jasper doesn't need you."

Ty removed the splints from Bergamen's leg, and then he moved his hands along the leg until he found the break. He sent his magic into the break.

"Hey," said Bergamen. "My leg's getting all warm, and it tingles."

Blossom smiled and said, "Those are your bones knitting back together."

After a few minutes, Ty moved his hands and then looked at Blossom. "Would you check that for me? I think his leg is healed."

Blossom examined the leg, as did Dr. Brunfeld. "That's remarkable," said Dr. Brunfeld to Ty. "It was a real honor to watch you, both with Jasper's back and with Bergamen's leg."

Queen Elicia pulled a bellpull in the corner of the room as she said, "Ty will need food after all that healing, and I suspect others are also hungry."

When a maidservant answered the bell, Queen Elicia said, "Felicity, could we have supper brought in here?"

"Certainly, ma'am," said Felicity, and she hurried out of the room.

Felicity was back in just a few minutes, pushing a cart that was heavily laden with foods of all kinds. Queen Elicia said, "Thanks. We'll serve ourselves."

Queen Elicia filled a plate and handed it to Ty. The others went to get their own food, and as always, King Bertram was amazed by his wife's abilities. She'd provided nuts and acorns for Samantha, dried meat for the dragons and foxes, and an assortment of stews and sandwiches for the humans. Once everyone was fed, King Bertram asked Ty about Claude.

"I'm guessing that Irene has filled in most of the information for you. Claude apparently grew up in the capital and went about setting up a loan agency that he used to enslave a good portion of the population. He's also been buying or trading the lands you opened up after the four barons were displaced. He now apparently owns or controls most of it."

"We need to put a stop to that," said King Bertram firmly. "I'll get my soldiers on it in the morning."

Esme let out a cry. Everyone turned her way, and Ty said, "What is it?"

"I've managed to access Jasper's thoughts, and they aren't good. He isn't fighting the poison. He doesn't think there's any point to fighting, because his father will just come after him again."

"No!" cried Bergamen. "He has to fight."

Esme shook her head and said, "According to Jasper, he's spent his whole life trying to be good enough for his father. He's thinking that he's never been good enough for anyone. Why else would his mother leave him?"

"But his father killed his mother," said Ty. "That wasn't Jasper's fault."

"According to Jasper, it was," said Esme. "If he'd been good enough, his father wouldn't have wanted to kill his mother. His mother wouldn't have had to protect him from his father if he'd been good enough."

"This poor boy," said Queen Elicia.

"How could someone have done this to him?" said Martha.

"We've got to make him want to fight," said Esme. "I don't know how to do that."

"Esme," said Ty, looking at her seriously, "you may be the only one who can. I remember a scared, abused young girl who felt much the same way that Jasper is now feeling. Do you remember? I bet Rupert and Samantha do. They saved you. What did you do, Rupert?"

We got her to remember the few happy times she'd had with us, and we sang to her.

"Esme, that's what you need to do for Jasper," said Ty.

"But I haven't known him that long," said Esme. "I don't know how to sing. I don't know what to say."

"Can you get Bergamen into your link with Jasper?" asked Ty.

"I can try," said Esme, "but Jasper isn't responding to me at all. I tried talking to him, but he wasn't responding. I don't think he even heard me."

"All you can do," said Martha, "is to try. No one is asking you to do miracles, but you're the only one who's able to read his intentions. Take Bergamen in with you, the way you and Jasper got into Rastan's mind. Jasper might sense Bergamen before he senses anyone else. They have a very close bond."

"Martha's right," said Blossom. "I've never seen a bond like Jasper and Bergamen's. It's worth a try."

Esme nodded and said, "I'll try. Bergamen, you'll need to stay calm for Jasper's sake. Don't get upset with him. He's had everyone in his life, at least since his mother died, upset with him."

"I understand," said Bergamen.

Esme and Bergamen linked minds, and then Esme returned to Jasper. Everyone in the room was absolutely quiet and still.

Esme said, *Jasper, Bergamen is here. He wants to speak to you.*

There was no response.

Jasper, I miss you. Ty has fixed my leg, so we can go move snow together. Remember all the fun we had with Wilhelmina? You learned how to move snow by telekinesis, and then we had snowball fights with Esme and Paul. You got so you could make snowballs with your mind and then send them flying. It was so much fun. I want to do that again. I want to go home and have some of Martha's fantastic stew. I need you. We've found such a good home in Dragonwind, and already we have lots of friends, and we have people who are counting on us. We are needed, and we are loved. Please, Jasper, can you hear me?

I remember feeling the way you do, Jasper, said Esme. *But now I love living in Dragonwind. Everyone is so kind. Please, fight this horrible poison. No one thinks you deserve it. Everyone agrees that your father is a terrible person. Trust me, no one could ever have pleased him, and you were so very brave to save Bergamen's egg. I wouldn't have been able to do that. And Bergamen loves you. The bond the two of you have is unique, the first of its kind in our world. You even convinced Sapphire that dragons need to end their isolation. You are a powerful force for good. Our world needs more like you. You can survive this. Things will get better, I promise you.*

Still there was absolutely no response from Jasper. Dr. Brunfeld checked him again, listening to his heart and breathing. Then he shook his head and said, "There's been no change. I think we have no choice but to try more of the antidote. If we don't, he will surely succumb."

Martha and Blossom looked at Jasper and finally nodded in agreement. Dr. Brunfeld motioned to Ty again to hold Jasper's head as he dribbled more of the antidote into his mouth. This time, it seemed to Ty that Jasper did swallow it more willingly.

"That's all we can do for now," said Dr. Brunfeld.

Esme stretched out next to Jasper and held his hand. Bergamen sat on the floor next to Jasper and put his head on Jasper's chest.

Everyone else found the most comfortable spots they could and kept vigil along with Esme and Bergamen. No one even thought about leaving the young man alone. There wasn't anyone in the room who didn't want to wring Rastan's neck.

▲

The night passed, and as dawn broke Dr. Brunfeld woke and checked again on Jasper. Esme and Bergamen had both fallen asleep, so he was careful to move around them without waking them. After his exam he walked over to Ty, touching him on the shoulder to wake him.

"What do you think?" said Ty.

"He's no worse," said Dr. Brunfeld, "which is something of a miracle in itself. I think we should try another dose of the antidote."

"OK," said Ty, standing up and stretching his stiff body. He followed Dr. Brunfeld over to Jasper and gently lifted Jasper's head so that Dr. Brunfeld could administer more of the antidote. Jasper swallowed it easily, which was a plus.

Wilhelmina looked up and said, *How's he doing?*

Ty said, "He's no worse, at least. We've just given him more of the antidote."

I don't know why I didn't think of this before, Wilhelmina said, *but I think we should get into Rastan's head and taunt him, saying that once again he's failed to kill Jasper.*

"How will that help?" asked Esme, who had awakened.

I think that Rastan might let something slip about what poison he used. I know that we have what we think is the antidote, but maybe it's missing something, some key ingredient. It can't hurt to taunt Rastan, and it just might get us more information.

Bergamen was listening. "I think maybe you have an idea, Wilhelmina, and I could pretend to be so excited because Jasper has recovered that I just wanted to let Rastan know he'd failed again. Coming from me, he might buy it."

I like your style, Bergamen. Let's do it. Esme, Bergamen, link with me, and I'll go find him.

Once they were linked, it took several minutes for Wilhelmina to find Rastan. *I don't know where he is,* she said, *but I have his thoughts. He's so pleased with himself.*

He won't be in a minute, said Bergamen. *Hey, Rastan! You're a real failure. Jasper is here, and he's alive and well. He's going to make sure that Claude knows where you are. He's tired of you trying to kill him.*

What do you mean he's alive? I gave him a triple-strength poison. He can't be alive. I even put in a secret ingredient to make it more powerful.

Sorry to disappoint you, said Bergamen. *Martha keeps all the best herbs on hand. We had no problem with the antidote. You really are the stupidest man alive.*

No, said Rastan, *you can't have gotten it in time. Why isn't he talking to me?*

You think he wants to talk with you after all you've tried to do with him? He's tried all his life to please you, and all you've done is whip and beat him. Well, he's found family now, real family, family that cares about him, so he'll never again talk with you. I'm just supposed to let you know that you've lost. You're weak, a real coward, and a disgrace to mages everywhere.

As Wilhelmina broke the connection, she noticed that everyone in the room was now awake.

"Did it work?" asked Ty.

"Yes," said Bergamen. "but there's a secret ingredient. He didn't say what it was."

Esme said, "He seemed to be thinking about the stream that comes down from the aerie."

Martha said, "There's lots of celery roots along that stream."

Dr. Brunfeld said, "Celery roots, as I'm sure you know, Martha, are used in a number of potions to make them more effective. I have some dried roots. I'll add them right away, but fresh would be better."

Criseda said, "I'll fly there right now. Can you describe these roots to me?"

Martha spoke up. "If you'll bear me, I'll go with you and show you. That would be the easiest and fastest way."

"Let's go, then," said Criseda.

Martha smiled and looked at Ty. "I find I'm enjoying riding dragons. We'll be back as soon as we can."

"Meanwhile, I'll add the powered roots to our current antidote and give Jasper some more," said Dr. Brunfeld.

▲

It took Criseda and Martha nearly three hours to get to the aerie and back. Martha had picked all the roots that she could find, many more than they needed, but there was no sense in taking the chance of not having enough.

As soon as they returned to the palace, Dr. Brunfeld took the roots from Martha and prepared them before adding them to the antidote. As soon as the fresh roots were added, the antidote began to bubble.

Dr. Brunfeld and Ty immediately administered it to Jasper. At first there was no change, but then Jasper took a really deep breath and sighed. He didn't wake up, but Esme said that he was trying to reach out telepathically. Bergamen called to him. *Jasper, can you hear me?*

Bergamen, is that you?

Who else would it be? You've had a really tough time, but you're going to be OK now. You're at the palace, and lots of friends have been very worried about you.

I have friends here?

Yes, you knucklehead. Ty and a bunch of others rescued you. Esme's been trying to get you to wake up. Wilhelmina tricked your father into giving us a missing ingredient for the antidote.

Esme broke in. *Don't you let him fool you, Jasper. The idea was Wilhelmina's, but it was Bergamen who taunted him so much that he spilled what the special ingredient was.*

Jasper actually smiled, and everyone in the room breathed a big sigh of relief. Dr. Brunfeld went over to Jasper and checked his pulse, temperature, and heart rate. As he finished, Jasper opened his eyes. "Who are you?" asked Jasper.

"I'm Dr. Brunfeld, and I'm very happy to meet you."

Dr. Brunfeld turned to the crowded room and said, "I think he's going to be just fine. He'll need a lot of rest, and feeding, but I think Martha can provide all that he needs. He should not travel for a week or so, but if he can stay here…"

"Of course," said King Bertram.

"Definitely," said Queen Elicia. "The boys will love to meet him and Bergamen."

With that, the group began congratulating Jasper and then making the arrangements to stay. It was decided that everyone from Dragonwind, along with Irene and Jennie, would stay in the palace. Dr. Brunfeld and Roland thanked the king and queen for their hospitality, told Jasper how glad they were that he'd survived yet another brutal attack, and left. They promised to check in to see how he was doing in a day or so.

CHAPTER 19

HOMECOMING

The next week was mostly peaceful. The palace buzzed with the activities of young people. King Bertram and Queen Elicia's four oldest children were happy for the company. Raymond, who was seventeen, played board games with Jasper and Esme, and the three became good friends. Raymond was a sensitive and intelligent boy, like his father, and he was very intrigued by Jasper's knowledge of dragons and magic. He also thought Jasper was very lucky to have Bergamen. He knew about Esme and her talents, and he was fascinated by her relationships with Rupert and Samantha, but somehow a dragon seemed even more wonderful.

Lance, who was eleven years old, watched the older youths, and after several days, when Jasper was feeling better, the four of them and Bergamen played hide-and-go-seek all through the castle. There were so many places to hide that even though the boys knew the castle better than Esme, Jasper, and Bergamen, they didn't have much of an advantage.

Six-year-old Jennie was a bit older than the five-year-old twins, Harriet and Hazel, but she was happy to look after them and supervise tea parties for their dolls and stuffed animals, including Earnest, as well as many of their games.

Irene, Martha, and Elicia enjoyed the chance to converse and share. Elicia told Irene about the opportunities she might have in the capital now that she was away from Claude, and Martha told her all about life in Dragonwind. Elicia had never been to Dragonwind, so she also enjoyed all of Martha's stories. Irene thanked them both for their information and said, "I think we'd like to resettle in Dragonwind."

Ty and Bertram conferred about the problems Claude presented. The day Jasper woke up, Bertram sent armed troops to arrest Claude. Ty went with them, and while they discovered that he'd fled the city, Ty did find his records, which he hadn't had time to take.

"We'll get him, sire," said Ty. "Not only do we now have all his financial records showing who owed him money, I also found the listing of his land holdings."

"Excellent," said the king. "I'll have all those lands confiscated, and it's likely that he has fled to one of those holdings as well. We'll find him. I'll send Simion and his troops to search all of Claude's holdings."

Three days later the capital was shaken by a strong tremor. Ty and Criseda went out to survey the damage, and they discovered that the only real damage was in the poorer section of the city. In fact, Claude's home was now nothing more than a heap of rubble, and there was a big hole around it where the tunnels had all collapsed.

At first Ty thought that Rastan was responsible for the earthquake, but then he talked to those who lived nearby and who were there when Claude's house and tunnels collapsed. They said they'd seen Claude leaving just before an explosion went off. Ty then concluded that Claude had blown up his home to cover up his activities. He obviously didn't realize that his files had already been removed and the drawers in his office were all empty.

Ty reported to the king telepathically. *This wasn't one of Rastan's earthquakes. It seems that Claude blew up his own home to protect himself, not realizing that all his files had already been removed. But there are major holes in the streets here, and some of the neighboring buildings were also damaged in the explosion, so I think these people need help.*

I'll send a crew right away, said King Bertram.

Ty and Criseda headed back to the palace after reassuring the citizens near the blast that help was on the way.

▲

At the end of a week, Dr. Brunfeld cleared Jasper for travel. After saying goodbye to the king and queen and thanking them for all their hospitality, the Dragonwind folks got ready to leave. Esme, Irene, Jennie, Rupert, and Samantha rode on Wilhelmina. Jasper and Bergamen rode on Criseda with Ty. And Blossom and Martha flew together.

Criseda and Blossom landed in Dragonwind an hour later. It took Wilhelmina a little over four hours to make the trip, but soon they were all back home. They received a rousing welcome from Kyle, Naomi and Paul, Jeb, and many others.

They were just settling back into their usual routine when a snowstorm hit. Jasper summoned up his magic and pushed the clouds away the way he had been, but right after doing that, he nearly collapsed from exhaustion.

"I guess I'm not as strong as I was before," he said as he sat on Martha's couch.

"You just wait," said Martha. "I'll feed you up, and you'll be good as new in no time."

Martha bustled into the kitchen and a short while later returned with Jasper's favorite, a thick, rich beef stew. Once he'd finished it, she insisted that he take a nap, and Jasper didn't resist. He was tired.

He was just starting to fall asleep when his father attacked him telepathically. *You think you got away from me, don't you? You were lucky with the antidote. But I have more ways to get you now. I've been looking for assistance, and now I've found several villagers who hate you as much as I do. They know you are a worthless piece of garbage, and they're going to help me get rid of you and that miserable excuse for a dragon. Then they're going to help me attack the dragons. I don't need Basil. He ran out on me. Too afraid of Claude, just because we owe him money. But Claude will never find me. He can have Basil. So don't get too comfortable. And my new friends are going to get rid of anyone who tries to help you. You can't stop us.*

Once his father left his mind, Jasper was shaking and sweating. Esme came running into his room and said, "Your father was here, wasn't he?"

Jasper could only nod.

"I felt him," said Esme. "He's nearby. And he's not alone."

"He says he now has friends in the village, friends who are going to kill me and anyone else who helps me."

"Well, he's just not going to succeed," said Esme. "I'm going for Ty."

As she left the room, Bergamen came in. "I felt him too," said Bergamen. "Why does he hate us so? Why is he trying so hard to kill us? It doesn't make any sense. Sure, you can push his clouds out of the way, but he can still mess with the weather. And he could do it anywhere he wanted—say, the capital, and we're too far away to change that. We really aren't any big threat to him, so why does he want us dead?"

Ty walked in just then, and he said, "I've been wondering that as well. It could just be his ego, that he can't stand anyone who messes with his plans, but I don't think so. And how was Claude able to control both Rastan and Basil? Claude doesn't have any magic at all. It wouldn't have been hard for them to get out of his influence. There must be more to this than we're seeing."

"I don't know," said Jasper miserably. "It sure doesn't feel good to know that someone hates me so much. And to know that it's my father only makes things worse."

"He hates me," said Bergamen, "but then, he hates all dragons. And I'm not very fond of him. He killed both of my parents."

"I'm very concerned with his comment that he now has friends to help him get to you," said Ty. "I suspect that they are the guys who left the village a while back. But it does seem as if there are those who aren't comfortable with magic, or at least with anyone who's different. Gorst and his friends left, but several of their wives stayed. Those who stayed seemed fine with differences, as far as I was able to tell."

"So do you think it's Gorst and his friends that my father has hooked up with?"

"It could be, or there could be others in the village who have just kept quiet. I'm not sure. But we do know lots of villagers who wouldn't work with Rastan. Most of the villagers, in fact," said Ty.

Esme returned then and said, "I also found Wilhelmina, and she thinks we should try reading Rastan's intent again, not only to find out what his plans are for Jasper, Bergamen, and the dragons, but also to find out why Claude had a hold on him. There's something weird going on. You're right about that, and we need to know what that is."

"I agree," said Ty. "I know he's watching the village, but I don't know from where."

"Let's go work with Wilhelmina. I'm too keyed up now to sleep," said Jasper.

▲

They found Wilhelmina at Paul's house. Naomi made them some tea and gave them cookies, and then they got down to work. Paul and Naomi headed out to the bakery to give Jasper, Bergamen, Wilhelmina, and Esme room to work.

Once they were all linked, Wilhelmina began searching for Rastan. It took her only a few minutes to locate him telepathically. She wished it were as easy to locate him physically. She took the other three with her into Rastan's mind. Esme went right to work trying to figure out his intentions.

Rastan was in the middle of talking with Gorst. Rastan wanted Jasper and Bergamen killed immediately, but Gorst wanted more money. Esme kept digging deeper into Rastan's intentions. She discovered that Rastan was angry and terrified. He was angry at the dragons for killing his great-great-grandfather and stealing their land, and that was why he wanted to kill them all. In addition, he also was terrified that Claude would come after him, but Esme couldn't find out why Claude terrified him. Suddenly Esme discovered why Rastan wanted Jasper and Bergamen killed so badly. He knew that between them they'd become very powerful magically.

Esme said, *Wilhelmina, let's get out of here.*

Once they were out of Rastan's mind, Wilhelmina asked, *Jasper, Bergamen, did either of you pick up anything?*

Jasper said, "My father is supposed to pay this guy to kill us. And he's supposed to kill us tonight."

Bergamen said, "I got that too, but I also got the idea—I don't know if it's true—that Rastan is really scared."

Esme then said, "You are both correct. I got a bit more as well. He's very scared of Claude, but I don't know why. I'd think that Rastan is more powerful than Claude, but I'm guessing that magic isn't the only kind of power someone can have. It would be good if we could figure out what Claude's hold over Rastan is.

"He's also trying to get Gorst to kill Jasper and Bergamen tonight. I'm not sure why the rush, but Gorst won't do anything until he gets paid. But we knew all that from what Rastan said to Jasper. What I did find out that's new and that I don't really understand is the reason he needs to kill both Jasper and Bergamen.

"Apparently, he has knowledge, or thinks he does, that when Jasper and Bergamen mature, they are going to have a combined magic, some kind of magic that they can only do as a pair. It's this combined magic that Rastan fears."

*I wonder...*said Wilhelmina. *Bergamen, did your mother say anything about a new kind of magic?*

"Not really," said Bergamen. "She did say that the bond between Jasper and me would be uniquely new. That it hadn't happened before and that we'd be misunderstood. But we've already experienced that. I don't remember anything about special magic or about us having a combined magic."

"I think we need to see Sapphire," said Esme. "I think that we need to learn more about magic in general."

"If we go to the aerie, then we'll be safe from Gorst and Rastan," said Bergamen.

"That's true," said Esme. "Let's see if Ty and Criseda can take us."

They found Ty at Martha's and updated him on what they'd learned. Then they asked him to take them to see Sapphire.

CHAPTER 20

AERIE

Ty and Criseda took Jasper, Bergamen, and Esme to the aerie to see Sapphire. Sapphire welcomed them. "How may I help you?"

Ty explained what Esme had learned from Rastan. "We have several questions. Windsong said that the bond between Jasper and Bergamen was unique. But does this unique bond have any magical properties? From what Esme learned, it seems that Rastan fears their combined magic, but they don't have any combined magic that we know of."

Sapphire smiled and said, "These two are unique among the current race of dragons. But remember, both your records and ours talked about the Ribendi, our forerunners, who helped humans. The Ribendi did not have magic, but as their ties with humans became closer, they changed, becoming more like today's dragons, and in the process they and their human friends began to develop magic."

Everyone nodded, and Sapphire continued. "Well, I've been studying the ancient records, and it appears that the Ribendi and the early dragons did have bonds like what Jasper and Bergamen now have. In fact, when the humans turned on the dragons and the dragons isolated themselves here, those humans who were bonded at the time came with their dragons to the aerie and lived out the remainder of their lives with their dragons. They couldn't bear to be separated. They also felt that the humans were in the wrong."

"So did those humans share magic with their dragons?" asked Ty.

"That's not as clear as I'd like it to be. Both humans and the Ribendi seemed to develop magic together. I'm now thinking, based on what's happening today, that magic grows when different species connect with each other. When the dragons and a few humans came to the aerie, well, some of the humans were male and some female, and as you might expect, there were children. But the dragons decided, in fairness to the humans, apparently, not to have any more dragon-human bonds. The next generation of humans then left the aerie and moved around the planet. It's my feeling that first generation of children are the ancestors of any humans living today who have magic, but I can't prove that."

Jasper said, "So all magic really arose from the close relationship of the Ribendi, the original ancestors of today's dragons, and humans?"

"I believe so," said Sapphire.

"Does that mean that there really isn't any difference between human magic and dragon magic?" said Jasper. "Can you also do weather magic?"

"Ah, I think I see where you're going, Jasper. Does this mean that we can 'outweather' your father, so to speak?"

Jasper nodded, and Sapphire said, "There are many different magical gifts. Ty, for instance, has the gift of healing, as does Blossom, but I don't. We all have magic, and whatever the form that magic takes, it all originally developed from Ribendi-human cooperation. But over the centuries, the forms that magic takes have varied. Currently, there are no other weather mages, at least not that I'm aware of."

"Telepathy seems to be the most common magical gift," said Esme.

"Definitely," said Sapphire. "That's probably due to the fact that the dragons refused to use human speech once the humans turned on them and the dragons moved to the aerie."

"Makes sense," said Esme. "And my ability to read intentions is like an empathic form of telepathy."

"I think you're right, there," agreed Sapphire.

"So what's the different or special magic that Jasper and Bergamen will develop?" asked Ty.

"That I'm not as sure of," said Sapphire. "In the ancient writings, it appears that when the human-dragon bond developed, that strengthened the magic that they each had. In this case, Bergamen will help Jasper's telekinesis get much stronger. Bergamen, you're too young to have developed your own talent, although you should be developing it soon, as you're nearly full grown. Whatever that talent is, it will be strengthened by your bond with Jasper. You both will share in each other's magic, in other words."

"And that's what my father is afraid of?" said Jasper.

"It would seem so," said Sapphire. "It's very sad on lots of levels that Rastan killed Windsong, because her real talent was in being able to see the future. We could really use that skill."

"Maybe that will be mine," said Bergamen.

"Dragons do sometimes share the same gift as their parents," said Sapphire. "For example, Blossom's mother was a renowned healer. But it doesn't always work that way. I was Windsong's mother, and I have no ability to read the future."

"You were Windsong's mother?" said Ty.

"You're my grandmother," said Bergamen.

Sapphire nodded and then said, "Unfortunately, I didn't handle our differences well at all. I pushed her away. I found her to be too stubborn. Mothers and daughters don't always have an easy bond, unfortunately. Not a day goes by that I don't regret my actions. But I hope to make that up to you, Bergamen. I really do."

"So Windsong could see the future," said Ty, "and she moved away from the aerie because she felt that dragons needed to come back into this world. Is that correct?"

"Yes," said Sapphire. "And I didn't believe her. I just thought she wanted more freedom to do her own thing. We fought a lot, and I think, now, that I drove her away. I was a fool not to believe her. Now I can never tell her how sorry I am."

"Grandma," began Bergamen. Then he stopped and thought before he said, "Can I call you Grandma?"

"Yes, little one, you may," said Sapphire.

"Well, she knew you loved her. And she was sorry she had to leave. When Jasper and I were in danger, she told us to come here. She told me that you would protect us. I think that's the clearest indication she could have given that she knew you loved her and were sorry. It may have taken you a bit to let go of the old ways, but you have, and what's more, she knew you would. She loved you too."

"Thank you, Bergamen," said Sapphire. "I hope you are correct."

"What I want to know," said Ty, "is did she ever give you the reason for knowing that the dragons needed to go out into the world? Did she ever tell you what was going to happen?"

"She never told me," said Bergamen. "She just said that we were the first of the new bonding and that we'd be misunderstood and our lives would be hard, but that this was the new way."

"She could never explain to me either," said Sapphire, "which is one reason I didn't believe her. However, the truth is that she never explained the future. She said that telling us what was going to happen could change it. She just talked in riddles, and that made it even harder to deal with, I'm afraid. I suspect that of all the magical talents or gifts, the gift of prophecy is the hardest one to bear. For your sake, Bergamen, I hope that doesn't turn out to be your gift."

"So we have no idea why Windsong thought that dragons and humans needed to interact more," said Ty.

"Unfortunately, no," said Sapphire.

"And we also don't know why Rastan and Basil are afraid of Claude," said Esme.

"Hmmm," said Ty. "Sapphire, I think you said that everyone who has magic is a distant relation of those humans who moved here to be with their dragons when the humans threw the Ribendi out. Do your records trace those genealogies?"

"I can check with Driselda, our historian," said Sapphire.

"Personally, I'd like to know, because I don't remember anyone saying that my parents had any magic," said Ty.

"And my parents certainly didn't," said Esme.

"Magical gifts don't appear every generation," said Sapphire. "I do know that. I'm not sure about your family tree, Esme, but Ty, it was your great-grandmother who was telepathic."

"Could we talk with Driselda?" asked Criseda.

"Yes," said Sapphire. "Let's go see her now."

They walked out of Sapphire's cave and through the dragon complex to another cave at the far end of the aerie. "Driselda," called Sapphire. "Are you free?"

Driselda, a huge emerald-green dragon, came out of her cave and said, "What can I do for you?"

"We have some historical questions," said Sapphire.

"Do come in, then. I love historical questions."

The group entered Driselda's cave, where they discovered nooks and crannies filled with parchment scrolls.

"Now, what can I do for you?" said Driselda.

Sapphire looked at Ty and said, "Go ahead."

Ty nodded and said, "We've been talking about the Ribendi and the humans who bonded with them, in I guess the same way that Jasper and Bergamen here have bonded."

"Ah, yes," said Driselda. "I've been wanting to interview you two, but let's get the questions out of the way first."

"As we understand it," said Ty, "the Ribendi-human bonds resulted in the growth of magic. Those humans with magic were the ones who bonded with dragons. Is this correct?"

Driselda nodded and said, "Yes, that's quite correct."

"We also have been told," said Ty, "that the humans who have magic now may be descended from those humans. Sapphire says that my great-grandmother, for instance, was telepathic. Is this also correct?"

"Very true," said Driselda. "Dragons are powerful, and they can gift magic. It should also be noted that we can take it away as well. But since the Ribendi were treated so badly by humans and since we've chosen to live outside the human world, we haven't gifted any humans with magic. Some, like yourself, have inherited it from ancestors who originally developed magic."

"Do you keep records of the genealogies of those humans with at least the potential for magic?"

"Definitely," said Driselda. "It would be irresponsible of us not to. That magical gift could be misused, and it's our responsibility to prevent that."

Esme spoke up. "Do you know where I got my talent from?"

Driselda smiled kindly on Esme and said, "Your gift popped up after a five-generation gap. It came as quite a surprise. It was your great-great-grandmother who was both telepathic and empathic, and that's why you have this rare gift. I should tell you that there was talk of taking the gift from you because of your parents. But when we saw how you stood up to them, we knew you would be of great help to this world, so we waited. If you hadn't escaped and come to us, well, we were sorely tempted to rescue you ourselves."

Sapphire said, "That's true. But we were very reluctant to get involved in human affairs. When we discovered the nature of the threat to you, and indeed to our whole planet, then of course we supported Criseda's assistance."

"More than that," said Driselda, "we've been monitoring you, Ty, and your relationship to Criseda."

"What?" said Ty.

"True," said Sapphire. "I was worried that you two were becoming too close, but I think Windsong saw it as not only inevitable but beneficial. She never said anything, but whenever I brought up the topic with others, I noticed her in the background, just smiling. It seems my daughter was much wiser than I. She would not have been so foolish as to try to separate you. Again, my apologies."

Criseda smiled and said, "Sapphire, truly, we do understand, and it takes a good leader to admit when she's made an error. So please, don't worry about it. We don't yet know why the relationship between dragons and humans needs to change for the sake of the entire planet, but it will be a major challenge for dragons to discover a way to work in the world instead of outside it, and I can't think of anyone I'd rather have lead us on this path."

"Thank you," said Sapphire.

"Back to the genealogies," said Ty. "Do you have a listing for all those humans who are now alive who do have magical gifts?"

"Of course," said Driselda. "And I should say that I've enlisted Wilhelmina's assistance in this matter, because there are several now who are problematic."

"Wait," said Sapphire. "You've had Wilhelmina working with you? Why didn't you tell me?"

"My concern hadn't reached that point until recently, and by then you seemed to be on top of things. I had Wilhelmina watching for Rastan and Basil. Until this last kidnapping, Basil hadn't done anything noteworthy. Rastan was a beastly parent, and I could tell that Jasper was much stronger in magic, or at least he will be, than Rastan, probably because his mother also had magic, inherited from her grandmother. Her family, along with a small colony of their friends, fled from a country far to the south of Estrea many generations ago and settled here. One of her distant ancestors had bonded with a Ribendi and moved to the aerie when the humans turned on the dragons."

"What was my mother's magic? And was she ugly, with dark skin like mine?" asked Jasper.

"No, she was very beautiful, as you also are," said Driselda, "and loving and kind. She had a darker skin, like all of her people, but it was very lovely, and you take after her. She had a special magic of being able to heal the spirit of people, making them less angry. It was an amazing gift, and she tried to use it on Rastan. Unfortunately, she wasn't able to turn him, but while she lived she did protect you. And so I waited to see what would happen.

"I was heartbroken when Rastan killed her. She didn't abandon you, Jasper. She ran from Rastan to save you. I couldn't do anything. Once she was gone, I again merely watched, as Rastan was all that you had. Until Rastan started hitting us with major snowstorms, he hadn't done anything that I could charge him with, as far as magic was concerned. Unfortunately, you are far from the only abused child in the world, although you are currently the only abused child with magical powers, since Esme is now safe. Still, that wasn't enough. But it was enough for me to have Wilhelmina keep an eye on things. Sorry I couldn't do more, Jasper."

"I understand," said Jasper quietly. "And if you hadn't had Wilhelmina looking out for us, well, Bergamen and I would be dead, so thanks for what you did do."

Driselda bowed to him. Then Ty asked, "Are there any other humans who are...what did you say, problematic?"

"Actually, yes," said Driselda. "There is a family that I'm growing concerned about. There's a father and son who have the gift of prophecy and far-seeing, and if I'm right, they've been abusing those gifts. I think they've been forcing Rastan and Basil to do things for them."

"Would the son's name be Claude?" asked Jasper.

"No," said Driselda. "There is a second son in the family whose name is Claude, but he has no magical talents at all. However, he is a tremendous bully, and he's getting rich from the information he gets from his father and older brother."

"Ah," said Ty. "That's why Rastan and Basil are afraid of Claude. A picture is beginning to form, and I can't say that I like it at all."

Driselda nodded and said, "I agree. You were very wise to get Irene and Jennie out of the capital and moved to Dragonwind. I would suggest that you talk with Irene. I think she knows, or suspects, more than she has so far divulged."

Sapphire said, "Windsong was always very careful with her gift not to let on to anyone what the future might bring."

"That's because she was a responsible far-seer. When this gift lands with the corrupt, it is inevitably a disaster. Ty, you messed with the time line. You had no idea that that's what you were doing, but Claude's father, Durkin, and his older brother, Clyde, had plans for that mother and daughter, and you've upset those."

"Good," said Ty.

"I have to agree," said Driselda, "but there will be consequences. In addition, you've brought little brother Claude to the attention of King Bertram. This will also have consequences."

"I understand," said Ty. "It would seem that we need to get back to Dragonwind and talk with Irene."

Sapphire said, "And I think we also need to have a larger dragon presence in the human world. Criseda says that the two of you are looking for a cave to share. Is that correct?"

"Yes," said Criseda. "Ty's cave is too small for a dragon. We've been so busy, and there's been the rather time-consuming problem of all the snow, but yes, we are going to find a space we can share."

Sapphire said, "Good. And please remember, you are always welcome here, both of you. I was thinking also of having Blossom spend more time in Dragonwind. She seems to get along really well with Martha."

Ty laughed. "I never thought Martha would take to riding a dragon, but now it's all she can talk about."

Sapphire chuckled and said, "I've always known that Martha has hidden depths. Well, here are my thoughts. Bergamen needs a teacher, one who can teach him what it's like to be a dragon. He also needs someone to help him develop his weak wing as much as is possible. Jasper needs schooling as well, but I assume Martha has someone in mind for that."

Jasper gave a small groan. "Yes, she does. Esme's tutor, Elfrida, wants to tutor both me and Bergamen."

"Elfrida's great," said Esme. "You'll like her. Just give her a chance."

Sapphire went on. "Ty, if you're going to be looking for a bigger cave, could Blossom have your cave? I think it would suit her, and she doesn't need a lot of space. It would put her close enough to help Bergamen, and Jasper as well, since you, young man, need to learn about dragons, just as Bergamen needs to learn about humans."

"I think that would be fine," said Ty, smiling at the look of worry on Jasper's face. "And don't worry, Jasper. This won't be anything at all like what your father did to 'educate' you. I think once you get used to it, you will enjoy it."

"OK," said Jasper. "If you say so."

"Good," said Sapphire. "That's settled. Now you all better be getting back to Dragonwind."

CHAPTER 21

THREATS

A s soon as the group returned to Dragonwind, they went immediately to find Irene. She was in the village hall helping Martha.

Ty said, "Irene, we need to talk with you. I'm hoping you can help us out."

"Certainly, Ty," said Irene. "I'm happy to help with anything you need."

"What do you know, or what have you heard, about Claude?" said Ty.

"Well," said Irene hesitantly, "I don't really know anything, and I'm not sure how much of what either he's said or others have said is true, as opposed to just bragging, but the rumor is that Claude's father is going to overthrow King Bertram and become king himself."

"What?" said Esme.

"It's just a rumor," said Irene. "But Claude kept telling me that his family is really powerful, that his father and his brother could take over the country, and that I'd do well to stay in his good books so that I could benefit from the change in governing."

"Did you believe him?" said Ty.

"I believed that he believed it," said Irene. "Now that I've met King Bertram and his wife, well, I would do anything to help them. I didn't think it would really make a difference to me who was king, but when I saw how kind they were to Jasper and how concerned they were for him and how they took Jennie and me in just because you asked them to, and they really seemed to care about us as well, then I started to realize that I wouldn't want anyone to harm them."

"Did Claude ever say how his father was going to get the throne?" asked Ty.

"He said something about weather and that I should get lots of warm clothes," said Irene. "Oh, he also said his father had people working for him who were too dumb to realize that they weren't going to get the power they thought they were. He seemed to find that very funny."

"Do you know where Claude's father lives?" said Ty.

"No," said Irene. "I think it's in the capital, but I have no idea where."

Ty stood, as did Esme and Jasper, and he said, "Well, if you think of anything else, please let us know."

"I will," promised Irene, and she went back to helping Martha.

Rupert came into the hall and straight up to Ty. *King Bertram wanted me to let you know two things. First, they just found Claude's body on one of his estates. He'd been knifed. Also, it's now snowing heavily in the capital.*

"Rastan must be somewhere in the capital," said Esme.

"Yes," agreed Ty.

"But he's not strong or brave enough to kill Claude," said Jasper.

"I agree," said Ty. "I think Claude was always the weak link in his family's chain, and I suspect either his father or his brother killed him. If he'd been bragging to others the way he did to Irene, they wouldn't have been happy. Whatever they think they can do, it would need to be kept secret."

"So now we have no way to locate Durkin or Clyde," said Esme.

"Not necessarily," said Criseda. "Driselda didn't share all her talents with you. There's a reason she's the historian, and that's because she can detect magic if she's close enough. I suggest we ask her to fly with us above the city and see if she can find any traces of Durkin and Clyde there."

"That's a great idea," said Esme, and Ty agreed.

"Does King Bertram need help with the snow?" asked Jasper. "I could move the clouds if he wants, or move the snow, or whatever else he wants."

Ty smiled and said, "That's very kind of you, Jasper. I'll check. Maybe tomorrow we'll head to the capital, but for now, let's call it a day. I suspect everyone is tired."

▲

They all had a quiet evening. Martha cooked a lovely dinner, and Esme helped. After dinner everyone relaxed before they finally headed off to bed. They were tired after all the activity of the last few days.

Ty had just fallen asleep when he was awakened by a scream. He was on Martha's couch, and it took him a few seconds to figure out who was screaming. It was Esme, and she was yelling for help, running toward Jasper and Bergamen's room, with Rupert and Samantha following her. She flung open the door, and Ty could see a man wrestling with Jasper. Bergamen was using his claws to grab at the man's head, and Jasper was pushing the man away using his magic.

Suddenly, Jasper succeeded in getting far enough away to push effectively with his telekinesis, and he threw the man across the bedroom, where he crashed into the wall. Ty stepped in and hauled the man up, asking Esme to get some rope.

Ty looked at the man and realized it was Gorst. Then Ty looked at Jasper and saw blood—his right arm was bleeding badly. Esme arrived with the rope, and Ty took it from her and said, "Can you get Martha? Jasper needs help."

Esme took one look at Jasper, who had blood dripping down his arm, and raced for Martha.

Ty tied Gorst to a chair in the room and then turned to help Jasper. Martha bustled in with her medical bag, and between the two of them, they stanched the bleeding and got Jasper bandaged. Ty was able to heal the cut so that it didn't need stitching, but it was still going to be a very painful wound.

"So, Gorst, what were you trying to do?" said Ty.

"I was supposed to kill the boy and his dragon," said Gorst. "If I did, I was going to be well paid."

"We know that Rastan hired you," said Ty.

"Yeah, so? I figure the kid must really be bad news if his own father wants to kill him."

"And you don't have any problem with killing?"

"No," said Gorst. "Why should I? The kid and the dragon are both freaks. The world would be better off without him."

"You know what, Gorst?" said Ty. "You're the one that the world would be better off without."

"What are you going to do with me?" asked Gorst.

"I'm going to tie you up in Martha's shed, and in the morning I'll take you to King Bertram and let him decide what to do with you," said Ty.

Ty escorted Gorst out to Martha's shed and secured him. Then he returned to check on Esme, Jasper, and Bergamen.

"Esme, how did you know that Jasper and Bergamen were in trouble?"

"Bergamen called to me. Rupert and Samantha heard a ruckus going on in here, so I called for help first, and then we came in. But by then Jasper had solved the problem."

"Well, you all did a great job," said Ty. "Now we'd better try to get some sleep, because I want us all to go to the palace tomorrow. The situation, which was bad enough before, has now gotten a whole lot worse."

▲

The logistics of flying them all to the capital got complicated, especially since Bergamen was nearly full-grown but still unable to use his wings properly. And while he was on the small side for a dragon, he was still significantly larger than a human. They did ask Driselda to come with them, and she was eager to do so. Thankfully, she was also one of the largest dragons, bigger than even Sapphire, so she was able to bear Bergamen's weight and still fly.

"Besides," she added, "I'd like to get to know this young dragon, as he's quite unique."

Jasper and Esme rode on Criseda with Ty. Rupert and Samantha weren't happy about being left behind, but Ty asked them to keep an eye on the village and let him know if there were any other difficulties. That just left Gorst, and Blossom said she was willing to bear him, as long as he had no weapons and was secured. She wouldn't let him ride her. Instead, she carried him in her front claws.

When they arrived at the palace courtyard, which was knee deep in snow, Ty had one of the guards take charge of Gorst. The rest of them went to meet the king, who decided that with four dragons in the group, even if one of them was smaller than the others, the ballroom would be the best place to gather, as it was the largest room in the palace.

"Now, please tell me what you've learned," said Bertram.

"You're in danger," blurted Jasper.

Bertram looked startled. Ty put a hand on Jasper's shoulder and said, "Jasper's right, but let me tell you the story in order."

With that Ty shared what they'd learned from Driselda and Irene, how they'd found an even bigger threat than Rastan.

King Bertram thought for a few minutes after Ty finished, and finally he said, "You mean that Rastan isn't the main villain? That this Durkin is, and that we have no idea where he is? And that he has magic that can tell the future, a future that he says means he will be king?"

Driselda said, "That's about it. But I think it's important to put his talent in perspective. It's true that the gift does have a foretelling quality, but what's vital to remember is that the future that Durkin sees is by no means guaranteed."

"Can you explain that?" asked King Bertram.

"Certainly," said Driselda. "Windsong, whom you may know was Bergamen's mother, had the same gift. However, she used it wisely. She never revealed what she saw. She did try to stop anything bad that she did see as a possibility. It's important to remember that they were just possibilities. My guess is that she saw what Durkin, with the aid of Rastan and Basil, was going to do. That she saw what Durkin sees. The difference is that she worked to prevent it, whereas Durkin sees it as his destiny. She realized that to stop Durkin, we were going to need to have dragons and humans working together. To that end she mated with Ventus, whose talent was premonitions, which is like foretelling but more immediate, and Bergamen was born. She knew he'd be orphaned, thanks to Rastan, so she taught him much more while he was in the egg than is customary for dragons.

"She also knew Jasper and saw what a fine young man he was. She realized that Bergamen and Jasper were well suited to each other, as Ty and Criseda are, and she ensured that they would be able to bond in a way that hasn't happened since our ancestors were friends with humans. My belief is that she's given us the tools we need to defeat Durkin and company. We just need to figure out how."

"So all this foretelling doesn't mean that the future is set, that we are fated to play it out?" said Bertram.

"Definitely not," said Driselda. "Our futures are still ours to determine, and what Windsong saw, what apparently Durkin has seen, is just one possible future. But it isn't the only one."

"DOWN!" shouted Bergamen.

Without even thinking, all of them dropped to the floor just as an arrow came through a window. It hit the wall just beyond where Bertram's head had been moments before. Guards rushed into the room, and Bertram said, "Find whoever shot that arrow."

Then he turned to Bergamen and said, "Thank you for saving my life. Did you see who shot the arrow?"

"No," said Bergamen, looking confused. "I just knew that an arrow would be shot at you. I don't know how I knew."

Driselda said, "It appears you have your father's gift of premonition."

"What's the difference between foretelling and premonition?" asked Bertram.

"They're really close, but foretelling usually is concerned with more distant events, and premonitions are things that will happen really soon," said Driselda.

"Why did it happen now?" asked Bergamen.

"You're nearly full grown now, and that's when most dragon gifts are awakened. I think you're also very clear about wanting to protect the king because of how he's cared for you, and your concerns over this latest development caused your gift to have a very timely awakening."

"Thank heavens," said Bertram. "And why is that window even open? It's too cold for open windows."

Bertram pulled a bellpull to call for a servant. When the servant entered, the king asked, "Why is this window open?"

"I don't know," said the servant, hurrying over to close it. "Gwen cleaned this room this morning. She knows better."

"Would you please call Gwen here?"

"Certainly, sire." And the servant left.

He was back a few minutes later with a young servant girl. She looked very nervous.

King Bertram smiled at her and said, "Gwen, can you tell me if you opened this window earlier today?"

"Yes, sir," said Gwen.

"Why did you do that?" asked the king.

"I'm not sure," she said. "It just seemed like the right thing to do. Did I do something wrong?"

Driselda spoke up then and said, "No, dear, but in future, if you think about doing something that you usually don't do, it would be best to ask the housekeeper if it's a good idea."

Gwen curtsied and said, "Yes, I will."

"Thank you, Gwen. That's all I wanted to ask," said King Bertram.

Once she'd left Driselda said, "Someone put a compulsion on her to obey their wishes. Their ability to command your servants raises the danger you face."

"Sire," said Ty, "may I recommend sending for Oscar and Foster to guard you and the palace?"

"Do you really think that's necessary?" said Bertram.

"After today's attempt, yes, I do," said Ty.

"Very well," said Bertram. "If Sapphire is willing, I agree. If nothing else, my boys will be happy to see them again."

CHAPTER 22

HUNTING

The group decided to stay in the capital until they either located Durkin or had to admit defeat. Driselda, with Esme; and Criseda, with Ty, went out on patrol every morning and stayed out until dusk.

Blossom stayed with Jasper and Bergamen. She was eager to see if there was any way that Bergamen could fly now that he was at the age when most dragons took their first flight. Lance and Raymond were eager to help with this project. Lance suggested that Bergamen launch himself off the second-floor balcony, but Blossom was quick to point out that if he couldn't fly, that could kill him. Lance said, "I guess that's not a very good idea."

"How will you test me?" said Bergamen.

"Let's see if we can find a large rock," suggested Raymond.

"That might be a good starting spot," agreed Blossom.

As they looked for a good spot where Bergamen could try launching himself without the danger of killing himself if he couldn't fly, Jasper kept an eye on the sky. Whenever he saw clouds forming, he pushed them off to the south, away from the capital, where their impact would be much less. After he'd done this three times, his father was shouting into his head, *Do you want me to be killed? Stop moving my clouds!*

Why should I care if you get killed? After all, you've done your best a number of times to kill me.

157

Don't you think if I'd really wanted to kill you that I would have succeeded?

But Jasper wasn't going to get hooked into that old argument. *You're always bragging about how powerful you are and how you're going to rule Dragonwind, but you aren't going to, are you? It's Durkin who's trying to rule, aided by his son Clyde. They've just taken advantage of your weather magic to further their plans. You're nothing. You won't rule over anything.*

Does it please you to see your father brought down?

Actually, no. It makes me very sad that you value power over the things that are really important. You've destroyed our family. You killed Bergamen's. Why? What for? Some vain ambition to rule? That's just sick. You're pathetic. You have nobody who cares for you. And now, if you don't do what Durkin wants, you could be killed. I truly pity you, but I won't let you hurt those I care about. I'll do everything in my power to stop you, said Jasper.

His father's voice held an edge of desperation. *You don't realize just how powerful Durkin is. He can tell the future. He knows what's going to happen before it actually happens. And Clyde can charm people, bend them to his will, make them do what he wants. Together they are unstoppable. They will win.*

You are weak and pathetic. Now get out of my head, said Jasper, and he gave his father a telekinetic shove.

Jasper then looked around, and he saw Bergamen on a ledge overlooking a small gully. Jasper walked over to stand beside Lance and Raymond as Blossom gave some last-minute directions.

"Now, remember, Bergamen, you may not fly far, or even at all, but you might be able to glide so that you land safely and easily. Shall we try?"

"Yes," said Bergamen, and Jasper could hear both determination and fear in his dragon's voice.

"Good luck, Bergamen!" shouted Lance enthusiastically.

"You can do it!" added Raymond.

"No matter what," said Jasper, "I think you're the best dragon in the entire world."

Bergamen took a deep breath and then jumped off the edge of the gully. He spread his wings and then flapped them. He did fly for a few seconds, but he flew in more of a circle than straight, because his one wing was so much stronger than the other. Then he got tired, so he did as Blossom suggested and glided to the bottom of the gully.

"Hooray!" yelled Lance and Raymond.

"Great job!" called Jasper.

"Excellent first try," said Blossom.

"But now I have to walk back up there," said Bergamen in a discouraged voice.

"Hey, maybe I could use my telekinesis to bring you back up here," said Jasper. "Want me to try?"

"Could you?" asked Bergamen.

"I don't know," said Jasper. "Let me try."

As the others watched, Jasper attempted to lift Bergamen slightly and bring him up the hill. At first nothing happened. But then Bergamen flapped his wings as Jasper pulled telekinetically, and soon Bergamen was skimming the ground and gliding uphill.

When Bergamen reached the top of the hill, Blossom said, "You two are quite the pair. That was incredible. From both of you! Good job!"

Raymond said, "Do you think we could make a wing extension for Bergamen? Something so both wings would be the same size?"

"That's an excellent idea," said Blossom. "His smaller wing is plenty strong. We've been working on that, and Bergamen does his exercises faithfully. But aerodynamically, the smaller wing won't work the same as the other wing, and that's why he went in circles."

"Let's see if we can't design something for him," said Raymond.

The group headed back into the castle and began working on a wing extension or cover for Bergamen.

▲

Meanwhile, even after several days, Driselda, Esme, Ty, and Criseda hadn't found any sign of Durkin. They had picked up on the telepathic communication of Rastan, and they circled his location. But Ty had them stay up high, because he didn't want to spook Rastan. They noticed that Jasper was pushing any clouds away from the capital, and Ty figured that Rastan wouldn't be very happy about that. He suspected that Durkin wouldn't be very patient, and now the snow wasn't falling in the capital anywhere. It was falling on dormant fields to the south.

So for now they merely noted the spot where they thought Rastan was hiding. They planned to keep an eye on it in case Rastan left and led them to Durkin or Durkin showed up where Rastan was hiding. They found a good hiding spot where the four of them could observe Rastan's cave but not be seen.

Esme kept monitoring Rastan, and it wasn't long before she said, "Rastan is really scared. He knows that Durkin had Claude killed not only because Claude had told too many people about Durkin's plans, but because Claude had lost his business. If Durkin would kill his own son over his boasting that his father was going to be king, then Rastan knows that Durkin would kill him if he couldn't deliver the weather he'd promised. And now he can't deliver the weather because of Jasper."

"Do you think that Rastan might be willing to come under our protection?" asked Ty.

"I'll try to plant an idea," said Esme. "I'll suggest that he's on the wrong side in this situation."

Esme sent the idea to Rastan. *Maybe you don't want to kill Jasper but instead get him to help you.*

Nothing happened. Esme sent the thought several times, at five- or ten-minute intervals. She kept doing it, over and over again all through the day. Rastan was terrified, and he wanted to run. But he knew that Durkin would find him.

Late in the afternoon, Clyde showed up to the cave. Soon there was a shouting match going on. Clyde said, "My father says that you need to produce a very large snowstorm at the palace, and it needs to happen tonight!"

"I can't guarantee that," said Rastan miserably. "My son is there, and he's pushing all my clouds away as fast as I make them."

"Well, make them faster!" said Clyde. "If you don't and my father has to come up with another plan to invade the palace, well, let's just say you won't see another dawn."

"It's not my fault," whined Rastan. "I've tried to kill Jasper, but he's too strong for me, and his friends are even stronger."

"You know my father's going to kill *you* if you don't help him," said Clyde. "In fact, he's given me permission to carry out the job if you say you can't get the castle snowed in by midnight."

"It's not possible," said Rastan.

Clyde brought out a knife and moved toward Rastan. Rastan shrieked, "No," just as Ty grabbed Clyde from behind. Esme moved in with a rope, and between them, they quickly subdued Clyde.

Esme then turned to Rastan. "Do we need to tie you up also, or will you come with us willingly?"

"I'll come," said Rastan in a resigned voice. "It seems that's the only way I can stay alive is to change sides."

"So it would seem," said Ty. "I think it would be in your best interest to come to the palace and tell King Bertram all that you know."

"You'll be sorry, old man," snarled Clyde.

"You didn't give me any choice," said Rastan.

Ty secured Clyde onto Driselda's back, with Esme riding behind him. Then he put Rastan on Criseda, sitting him in front of himself. It didn't take long to fly back to the palace.

CHAPTER 23

INTERROGATION

King Bertram led the interrogation of Rastan and Clyde. Ty, Esme, Driselda, and Criseda listened. Clyde refused to say anything, but Rastan was eager to talk. He began. "I thought I could use weather magic to get rid of the dragons. They're too powerful, and I don't like them."

"That doesn't seem like a very good reason to kill off an entire species," said King Bertram.

"Well, I thought I was the most powerful mage around, and I wanted to rule Dragonwind, which used to belong to my family. I got Jasper and me out of the capital because Durkin was trying to make me work for him. I'd gotten into debt with Claude, and Durkin said if I worked for him, my debt would be forgiven. But Durkin is really scary, so we fled, and I figured I'd just get my family lands back," admitted Rastan. "Things started off well. I was able to capture two dragons and their egg. I killed the dragons one at a time, and I thought I'd destroyed the egg, but I had no idea that Jasper rescued it, although I suppose I should have. The boy is soft."

"Your son is a very fine young man with a good heart," said Ty.

"As I said, he's weak. Anyway, I thought things were going well, but then Durkin found me again. It seems that he can see the future, and what he saw showed me helping him to become king."

"That must have been a blow to your ego," said King Bertram.

"Well, whatever, he made it very clear that either I work for him, or I'd be killed. Not much of a choice, so I did what he told me. But once Jasper started to develop his powers, things went badly wrong. I could make the storms, but Jasper could move the storms to places where no one would be hurt. I kept trying, but nothing worked.

"I then kidnapped Jasper and hoped that I could then keep him from stopping my storms. Basil helped me with that, but as I'm sure you know, I ended up having to poison Jasper and run. Unfortunately, that didn't work either, and I couldn't get away from Durkin.

"Then Durkin sent an assassin, who got a servant to open a window, and then he shot an arrow, but again Jasper foiled the attempt. Durkin blamed me, but I had no idea that he had the gift of premonition!"

"He didn't," said Driselda. "That was Bergamen's doing."

"That runt of a dragon?" said Rastan.

"I wouldn't call him that if I were you," said King Bertram.

"Anyway, I got blamed for that failure also," said Rastan. "If I can't help Durkin, then I'm to be killed. After all, he killed his own son because he talked too much. He's not about to take any chances with me."

"You do seem to be in a tight spot," said Bertram. "And so far you haven't told us anything we didn't already know. If you want our protection, you have to tell us something new. After all, given what you have done to Bergamen, Jasper, and Bergamen's parents, we aren't inclined to show you any mercy."

"But I don't know anything!" wailed Rastan.

"Oh, I'm sure you do," said Bertram. "I could have my guards beat it out of you, but again, if I have to do that, I still won't feel kindly toward you. If you want our assistance, you need to cooperate with us."

"But I'll be killed," said Rastan.

"If Esme and I hadn't interfered, you'd already be dead. We saved your miserable life. So what are you going to do to earn that and stop us from just throwing you over a cliff?" Ty threatened.

"You wouldn't," said Rastan.

"I might," said Esme. "Jasper nearly died from the poison I saw you give him."

"But I had to," said Rastan as panic crept into his voice. "It was either him or me."

"I know parents who would willingly give up their lives for their children," said King Bertram. "In fact, Ty's parents did just that. You're a lousy excuse for a parent. You even killed Jasper's mother. So don't expect any sympathy from us. Give us some information, tell us all that you know, or my guards will beat it out of you and then throw you over a cliff."

"I don't know much," said Rastan.

"Shut up, old man," said Clyde.

"Oh, do you want to talk now?" said Bertram.

"Never," said Clyde.

Rastan looked at Clyde and then said, "Durkin, Clyde, and Claude grew up in the poorest section of the capital. Claude was a year younger than Clyde, and their mother died giving birth to him. Durkin and Clyde had magical talent. Durkin, as you know, could see the future. Clyde has the ability to persuade anyone to do just what he wants. But the most successful of the three was Claude. He might not have had magic, but he had a gift for making money.

"The three lived hand-to-mouth until Claude was about seventeen. Then he started making a lot of money by making loans at really high interest rates. He's been supporting his father and brother since then. Well, until they killed him. Durkin, especially, thinks he has a lot more power than he really does. He's even more of a narcissist than I am, and that's saying a lot.

"He was determined that he could become king. He was obsessed with wealth and power, probably because he'd lived his whole life without it. He saw others gaining wealth and influence, like some of your nobles, and he was going to gain more than anyone else. However, I suspect now, with Claude gone, that the little wealth he has accumulated will soon be gone," said Rastan.

"What do you know?" said Clyde. "We're going to take over this palace and rule, and then we'll have plenty of money. Just wait and see."

Rastan shook his head and said, "See what I mean? Durkin hasn't even noticed that his supposed future has changed over time. He thinks that the future he sees now, where he kills you and takes over Estrea, is the same future he saw when his sons were small. When they were small, he saw that he'd get power and wealth, but as a rich merchant, not as king. He didn't see himself as king until after he found Basil and me. He also doesn't realize that being able to read the future is more curse than blessing, especially if you believe that there's no way to change it. He doesn't think he can be stopped, which makes him vulnerable."

"What do you know?" said Clyde. "My father is brilliant."

"Yes, brilliant at deceiving himself," agreed Rastan. "My plan, my deluded plan, at least involved only my own talent. I am a very strong weather mage. I *can* control the weather. It wasn't sufficient, but at least it's real."

"You were defeated by your own son," said Clyde. "And he's just a boy."

Esme interrupted. "King Bertram, may I see you, now?"

"Certainly," said Bertram.

They stepped out into the hall, and Esme said, "Clyde is counting on his father rescuing him tonight. There's an attack planned for just after midnight."

"Thanks, Esme," said Bertram. "Let's lock these two in the dungeon and then get ready."

They went back into the room, and Bertram instructed his guards, "Take these two to the dungeon. Be sure they are securely chained to the wall and that guards patrol the dungeon corridors."

"Yes, sire," said the guards as they ushered Rastan and Clyde out of the room.

CHAPTER 24

ATTACK

Once the prisoners were gone, King Bertram looked at Ty, Esme, Driselda, and Criseda and said, "So, how serious is this talk of an attack?"

"Clyde certainly believes in it, and that it will be successful," said Esme. "He thinks it would have been nice if Rastan could have made a blizzard, but he doesn't believe that his father really needs it."

Henry knocked on the door and then entered. He said, "Sire, Oscar and Foster are now here. They'll guard the perimeter of the castle. They also asked me to tell you that Wilhelmina and Martha are on their way here. They should arrive this afternoon."

"Thanks, Henry," said Bertram.

As Henry left, Jasper, Bergamen, Lance, and Raymond, along with Blossom, came into the room. The group was obviously excited.

Bergamen shouted, "I can fly!" He turned around to show off his new wing.

Raymond said, "We did it! We designed a special addition to Bergamen's wing, thanks to a lot of help from Blossom, and we tried it out. Bergamen can fly really well. He gets tired easily, but he'll get stronger with practice."

Ty looked at the group and then said, "That's fantastic! Raymond, I've always thought you'd make a great engineer. Well done!"

"It will be a while before Jasper can ride on Bergamen," said Blossom, "but that will happen. Meanwhile, Bergamen has matured to the point that he can also now breathe fire. He's truly growing up."

Jasper ran his hand over Bergamen's back and said, "He's the best dragon. I can't wait until we can fly together."

Blossom said, "Just don't try it until I give the OK. You wouldn't want to hurt him."

"I understand," said Jasper.

King Bertram said, "I'm really impressed with all you have done for Bergamen. And I was just about to call for some of you, at least. The castle is going to be attacked tonight. We need to prepare to defend it."

"Wow," said Lance.

"Not 'wow,'" said Ty. "I suspect your father didn't mean to call you two into this conference, so if you plan to stay, you'd better listen and then help us plan."

"Yes, Uncle Ty," said Lance. Ty was an honorary uncle, not a blood relation, but the boys really looked up to him.

"We don't have any information about how Durkin plans to attack," said Bertram. "He asked Rastan to cause a blizzard tonight to disguise his attack, but thanks to Jasper, that's not possible. Durkin doesn't have any attacking powers of his own, so magic won't be involved in the actual attack."

"I have no idea how they think they can succeed," said Driselda. "After all, we have five dragons here, in addition to the regular palace defenders."

"Actually," said Criseda, "we'll have six dragons. I've just heard from Sapphire, and when she found out that we'd captured Rastan and Clyde and that Durkin would be here tonight, she decided to come. She's the one with the authority and ability to remove their magical talent, if that's what is decided."

"I have the feeling that we're missing something," said King Bertram, "because it does seem as if the attackers are not strong enough. Let's just be sure we're ready for anything."

▲

Wilhelmina and Martha arrived late that afternoon after their four-hour journey from Dragonwind. Martha said, "If the palace is going to be attacked, I thought you might need my nursing skills."

Wilhelmina said, *Sapphire told me what was going on, and I thought I'd like to be part of the defense. I was also able to capture Basil.* She dropped a large sack on the floor.

"You are both most welcome," said King Bertram. Then he motioned to the sack and said to one of the guards, "Can you make sure this prisoner stays unconscious until we can deal with him?"

"Yes, sire," said the guard as he lifted the sack and left the room.

Then King Bertram said, "The queen has arranged for dinner for all of us, so let's eat and then get ready for whatever comes next."

▲

After dinner, the queen took all the children upstairs to the private royal quarters. Lance and Raymond both protested loudly about being sent away until their father said, "So you expect Ernest to defend your mother, with the help of your sisters?"

Since Ernest was nearly three years old and the twins were only five, this was obviously an impossibility. Raymond knew his father wanted both him and Lance out of any danger, but he accepted the face-saving request. "No, father, of course not," Raymond said, and Lance nodded in agreement.

Once his family had left, Bertram said, "Any last-minute ideas? I'm still convinced we're missing something."

No one had any suggestions, so they waited. Jasper finally said, "I hate waiting."

Suddenly, Bergamen let out a cry. "The queen's in danger!"

Esme added, "Clyde is free. He persuaded the guards to let him go, undo his shackles, and open his cell. He's now in your private quarters, and he has a knife at Queen Elicia's throat. He's telling the girls to stop crying, and he's making Lance tie up Raymond."

"That's what I'd forgotten," cried Bertram. "The open window!"

Ty looked confused and then said, "Ah, yes. The parlormaid who opened the window for no known reason. Clyde's ability is compulsion."

"And that's how they plan to take the palace," said Bertram. "They know I won't let harm come to my family."

Martha said, "We just have to find a way to be sure they stay safe and Clyde and Durkin are caught. May I ask, is there a nursery maid with them?"

"I don't think so," said Bertram. "Elicia usually does the nighttime routine by herself. I help whenever I'm free. It's sort of our ritual."

"But Clyde wouldn't know that, would he?" asked Martha.

"I don't think so," said Bertram, sounding very confused.

"So if I knocked and entered, just the way a servant would," said Martha, "I could pretend to be the nursery maid come to put the little ones to bed."

"No," said Bertram. "That would just put you in danger as well."

"I may not have magic," said Martha, "but I've stopped villains before. And Esme can read me like a book, so I can at least get you more information."

"I don't like it," said Bertram.

"Neither do I," said Ty, "but she's the only one of us who could bring this off."

Martha stood up and headed to the door, saying, "One flight up, first door on the left?"

"Yes," said Bertram.

When she'd left, Jasper said, "Did my father get out at the same time?"

"Good question," said Bertram.

"No," said Esme. "Clyde didn't charm the guards to let Rastan out."

"Is there any way we can get Rastan to help us?" asked Ty.

Bertram rang the bell, and when a guard came, he said, "I need you to bring Rastan up here as quickly as you can."

It was only a few minutes before the guard was back with Rastan. The guard said, "Sire, the other prisoner is gone, and all the guards down there are unconscious. What should I do?"

"Nothing at the moment, but be ready to come if I call," said Bertram.

"Yes, sire."

Once the guard left, King Bertram turned to Rastan. "I hate to say this, but we need your help. Clyde is holding my wife and five children at knifepoint. I'd like to offer you a deal, if you're willing."

"Go ahead," said Rastan.

King Bertram looked briefly at Esme, and she nodded her understanding. She was to read Rastan's true intentions. Bertram said, "Do you know anything about Durkin's plan for tonight?"

"He's coming with a bunch of thugs," said Rastan. "They plan to arrive just after midnight. They're coming from his house, which is just on the outskirts of the capital."

"And he wanted you to make a blizzard, right?" asked Bertram.

"Yes, to disguise them."

"Could you drop the blizzard on them, near his house?"

"Sure," said Rastan, "but why should I?"

"Right now you're likely to be executed," said Bertram. "You killed your wife and two dragons and countless others; you attempted to kill your son and Bergamen several times. If you help us, I'll guarantee that you won't be killed and, further, that you won't be locked up. That should be worth something to you."

"Not to mention that Durkin and Clyde don't seem well disposed toward you," added Ty.

Rastan thought for several minutes. Finally he said, "You have a deal. When do you want the storm?"

"Now," said Bertram. "And we want it to hover over Durkin, blowing hard so they can't see."

Rastan nodded and set to work.

Esme said, "Martha's in the nursery. Clyde's not happy to see her, but he's allowed her to put Ernest and the twins to bed, so they're out of harm's reach. She says that both Lance and Raymond look murderous. She's noticed that there is slack in Raymond's ropes. Lance, apparently, didn't do much of a job of tying them. Unfortunately, Clyde still has his knife at Elicia's throat."

"If he hurts them, I swear I'll kill him," said Bertram.

"Can you get a read on Clyde? Or Durkin?" asked Ty.

"No, unfortunately. Wilhelmina, can you?"

I'm trying, said Wilhelmina. *I can sense a large group of men, and yes, they're in the middle of a blizzard. Oh, their language isn't very nice. They're calling Rastan lots of names for not hitting the right target. They are struggling through very high drifts.*

"Good," said Ty. "Now that Durkin and his thugs are slowed down, we need to worry about Clyde. Bertram, does the dumbwaiter in the nursery still work?"

"Yes," said Bertram, "but what good—"

"Give me a minute," said Ty. Finally he said, "Jasper, I really hate to ask you, but I think you're the only one small enough to ride in the dumbwaiter. Do you think you could get in and then use your telekinesis to disarm Clyde? Bertram and I will be right outside the nursery door, so you won't be alone with him for long."

"I can sure try, sir," said Jasper.

"OK," said Ty. "Come with me, and I'll show you the dumbwaiter and also explain the layout of the nursery."

Ty did as he said. He also told Jasper not to be heroic. He pulled the ropes to raise the dumbwaiter after telling Jasper not to open the door into the nursery until Ty told him that he and Bertram were in position.

Once Ty had raised Jasper to the nursery floor, he ran back for Bertram. The two of them slowly and quietly went up the stairs to the nursery floor. They immediately noticed that Martha hadn't closed the nursery door all the way, so they could see Lance and Raymond on the floor. Bertram caught the boys' eyes and motioned for them to be very quiet.

Ty gave the signal. *Your turn, Jasper.*

Jasper carefully opened the door of the dumbwaiter. He saw the boys staring at their mother. Jasper could see Clyde standing behind Elicia. The knife was right against her throat. Jasper was afraid that if he didn't time things just right, Clyde's hand would slip and cut Elicia.

Jasper took a deep breath and focused on the hand holding the knife. He gathered his telekinetic power, and then he flung Clyde's hand away from Elicia. As soon as he did that, Lance and Raymond raced for Clyde, just beating Ty and their father. It was all over in a moment. Ty held tightly to Clyde as Lance brought the rope he'd supposedly tied Raymond up with. Ty made sure that Clyde was tightly bound this time.

Martha came over and gave each of the boys, including Jasper, hugs and said, "You all were very brave. I know your parents are proud of you two, and

Jasper, I couldn't be any prouder of you if you were my own flesh and blood. Great job!"

▲

Sapphire landed in the palace courtyard. Criseda and Driselda went out to greet her, and Driselda said, "We've caught Rastan and Clyde. Clyde was holding Bertram's family hostage, but Jasper helped rescue them. Durkin is being harried by a blizzard that Rastan made at Bertram's request. I think that catches you up on the big points. Let's get inside before Durkin arrives."

"Sounds as if you barely need me," said Sapphire as they entered the palace.

"I wouldn't say that at all," said King Bertram. "How wonderful to meet you at long last. You've been so much help to me and my people."

"My pleasure," said Sapphire.

They entered the ballroom where Rastan and now Clyde were being held. Bertram said, "I promised Rastan that he would live and that he wouldn't be incarcerated. I had to give him something to get him to put a blizzard around Durkin, but I'm beginning to think that Rastan is seeing the error of his ways as well."

Esme nodded and said, "He'll always be a narcissist, but he's at least more realistic about what he can do and what he *shouldn't* do now."

Sapphire nodded and said, "Then I think just stripping him of his powers will be punishment enough."

"What?" yelled Rastan. "You didn't say anything about that!"

"I'm giving you everything I promised," said Bertram.

"I had no idea anyone could take away my powers," said Rastan.

"You'll be better off without the temptation," said Sapphire, "and at least you keep your life, and you won't be thrown in a dungeon."

Rastan nodded. Sapphire looked him square in the eye and then blinked. A small light flew out of Rastan's eyes. Jasper tried to contact him telepathically, but nothing happened. Esme looked into his mind and said, "He's nonmagical."

"It's not hard to do," said Sapphire. "At least not for me. It's a power that the leader of the dragons has. Now, what about this one?" She motioned to Clyde.

"He's another story," said Bertram. "I don't know whether he killed his brother or his father did, but he was going to kill my wife and family. He is able to compel people to do whatever he wants them to do."

"I think I'll not only take away his magic but also erase his memories. He can start over. I assume you have farms that could use cheap labor," said Sapphire.

"Definitely," said Bertram.

Sapphire stared into Clyde's eyes. He tried to duck his head, but she maintained contact. When she was done, she said, "So, who are you?" to Clyde.

"Huh," said Clyde. "I'm…I'm…I don't know."

"That will be sufficient," said Sapphire.

Bertram looked at the man who'd held his family hostage, and then he called a guard. "Take this man to the bunkhouse for now, and tomorrow take him to the farm cooperative and let them know he's available for work."

"Yes, sire," said the guard, leaving with a very puzzled Clyde.

Ty said, "Maybe you should pass sentence on Gorst now, while we wait."

King Bertram said, "Gorst tried to kill Jasper, I think you said."

"Yes," said Ty, "although he wasn't much of a threat. Jasper handled him easily."

King Bertram thought for a moment and then said, "I think I'll sentence him to work at the farm cooperative for five years."

Ty smiled and said with definite sarcasm, "Oh, he'll just love that."

CHAPTER 25

NEW ALLIANCE

"**S**o that's all but Durkin," said Sapphire. "What's the plan for him?"

King Bertram smiled and then said, "Well, they should be tired after moving through the blizzard. Wilhelmina has been tracking them. What's her latest report, Ty?"

"She says that they're nearly here," said Ty.

King Bertram nodded and said, "What about a show of dragons? We now have seven of you here, counting Bergamen. I'd think that would be pretty daunting for even the biggest bullies."

Sapphire chuckled and said, "And I understand that Bergamen is old enough now to breathe fire."

"And my sons, with Blossom's assistance and guidance, designed a wing extension for him. Wait until you see it. He's so proud that he can now fly," said Bertram.

Ty said, "He's a real testament to overcoming adversity. And Raymond will make a fine engineer, I think. His design is really pretty smart, and Blossom said she only gave a few suggestions."

"Lance and Raymond have certainly proved themselves today. They tackled Clyde before Ty or I could get near him. The minute Jasper moved the knife, they had Clyde flat on the floor and began tying him up. I'd made some statement to them when I insisted that they go to the nursery that they should protect their mother and younger siblings, and they obviously took that to heart," said Bertram with evident pride in his voice.

"Let's talk about this further," said Sapphire, "once we've taken care of Durkin. I have an idea or two I'd like to run past you."

"Wonderful," said Bertram.

Esme said, "I believe Durkin is now here. He doesn't seem to realize that anything is amiss."

"Thanks, Esme," said Sapphire. "Your front entry is quite large, Bertram. Let's fill it with dragons. Oscar and Foster can come in behind the group, and Bergamen, Blossom, Driselda, Criseda, and I will be in the front."

Once the dragons were ready, King Bertram opened the palace door and stepped aside.

"Time for you to give up your throne," said Durkin, and then he stopped dead in his tracks. "Wh-what's this?"

"This is the end of your reign of terror," said Sapphire. She stared deep into his eyes, then blinked, and a ball of light flew out of them. "I think you will now find that your magic is gone. No more foretelling; no more telepathy. And now," she said as she nodded first at him and then at his fifteen buddies, "no more memories for any of you."

The men became very bewildered, looking around, saying things like "Where are we?" followed by "Who are we?"

King Bertram laughed and called to his guards again. "Here are some more workers to be sent to the farm cooperative in the morning. Put them wherever you have space for tonight. They shouldn't cause you any trouble."

"Yes, sire," said one of the guards as he and his fellow guards removed the sixteen men.

"Well, I, for one, am tired," said King Bertram. "What do you say we call it a night and meet again in the morning over breakfast?"

Everyone agreed that this was a sensible plan.

▲

In the morning the palace staff set up a lovely breakfast buffet in the ballroom. There was plenty for everyone. Once everyone had their fill, King

Bertram said, "Now, Sapphire, I believe from some of the things that Ty has told me that you have something you want to propose."

"Yes, I do," said Sapphire. "I don't know how much you know about the history of humans with our ancestors, the Ribendi, but since the humans restricted us to the aerie, there has been very little interaction between the two races."

"I know that humans treated the dragons very badly and that we were lucky the dragons didn't retaliate," said Bertram.

"Driselda, why don't you let us know what you found?" said Sapphire. Then, turning to Bertram, she said, "Driselda is our historian."

Bertram nodded as Driselda began. "The Ribendi had a lot of knowledge, and they really helped the humans, but they did not have any magic. I've been trying to figure out just when magic entered this world, and what I suspect is that the magic developed as part of the chemistry between dragons and humans. As the dragons had more contact with humans, magic grew. That's also when the Ribendi developed into our modern dragons."

"Interesting," said Ty.

Driselda nodded. "We've also found that those humans who have magic today are actually descended from the humans who left the human settlements to go to the aerie with their dragons. They had relationships similar to Jasper and Bergamen's or Ty and Criseda's."

"Do you know who all these humans are? The ones who have magic?" asked Bertram.

"Yes, our records have traced the descendants of the original humans who were linked with dragons. I can tell you, for instance, that your great-great-great-grandfather was one of those humans."

"Wow!" said Bertram. "That's amazing."

Sapphire said, "That brings me to what I wanted to discuss. Magic apparently grows when dragons and humans have deep connections. In fact, given what you, Wilhelmina, have got with Paul, not to mention Esme with Rupert and Samantha, it may be that any connection between two species is magically potent."

"That would make sense," said Ty. "I was glad that my healing magic had grown stronger over the years, or else I might not have been able to save you,

Jasper, but I thought it was just because I was practicing. I didn't even think that it could be because of Criseda."

"We learned, I think," Sapphire said, "that we needed each other to solve this past crisis. In fact, we've needed each other every time we had a crisis. But why should we wait for a crisis before we work together? Wouldn't our society and, indeed, our planet be better off if we always worked together?"

"For sure," said Jasper. "And look what that working together has done. I mean, aside from taking care of the villains. Look at Bergamen. He can fly now. And that's thanks to Raymond and Blossom working together."

"Very true," said Bertram. "And I'm very happy for you, Bergamen."

"Exactly," said Sapphire. "That's why I'd like to propose an alliance between dragons and humans. I'd like to see us working together once more. I'd also like to see those like Raymond, who does obviously have not only great intelligence but also a keen interest in dragons and an exceptionally kind heart, spend time with us, possibly during the summer. Further, I'd like to send some of our dragons to spend time with humans. For instance, Blossom and Martha share an interest in healing methods."

Ty smiled and said, "And Driselda could work with Aloysius."

Bertram laughed and said, "He'd have to be willing to come out of his turret, because there's no way that Driselda could get up to him."

"This is what my mother said would happen. She said that Jasper and I would be the first human-dragon pair in this era but that we wouldn't be the last," said Bergamen.

"Further," said Sapphire, "dragons are not going to stay only in the aerie. Criseda and Bergamen have already moved out. I think, Bertram, that we'll need to look at all of Estrea and see where you might think dragons would be helpful."

"Certainly, and Durkin's plans have let me know that the poor section of the capital needs assistance. I was unaware of what those like Irene and Jennie were suffering. That situation needs to be addressed," said Bertram. "I think our alliance will be able to help a lot of people."

After a moment Ty said, "I agree, but we also need to be prepared for a backlash from those who will be upset by a change in the social order. There are those who consider humans to be the rulers, with all other species just here for our benefit. Even in Dragonwind, where folks are familiar with dragons, we keep having unpleasant encounters."

King Bertram said, "Can you give us a recent example?"

"Definitely," said Ty. "At the height of the snowstorms, before Jasper mastered sparing us from them but after he'd learned to move the snow to make paths, several of our village men told me that I needed to get rid of Jasper and Bergamen because they were the cause of all the snow.

"I pointed out that Jasper and Bergamen had nowhere else to go. The men didn't care. And they were so upset that they went on a more general rant, saying that we had too many unnatural and deviant things going on. He cited not only Jasper and Bergamen but also Wilhelmina's relationship with Paul, Esme's with Rupert and Samantha, mine with Criseda, and of course he didn't say as much, but I'm certain at the top of his list was my being changed to a male, when he knew I wasn't born with a male body."

"That's horrible," said King Bertram.

"Yes, but unfortunately it isn't that rare. People were stressed by all the snow. There was no doubt about that. You can't be landed with nine times the yearly average and not be stressed. When people are scared and worried, they tend to focus on things that are different. They're looking for someone to blame. They're also looking to reaffirm how normal they are. Unfortunately, it's a fairly common coping mechanism. It should be noted that none of the wives left when I told the husbands to get out of Dragonwind if they were worried by the snow. The wives seemed relieved that the men were gone, so I suspect they aren't the best representatives of our species. Nevertheless, I just felt we should be aware of what the backlash will be."

Driselda said, "Don't you think the alliance is a good idea?"

Ty smiled and said, "I think it's a wonderful idea. I'm all in favor of it. But just as Bergamen's mother warned him and Jasper that they were in for a rocky time, I want us to be prepared that not everyone will see it as a good thing. We just need to try to minimize the discomfort level of the average citizen. And honestly, I think when they see that we're getting rid of the bullies and scoundrels like Claude, most of them will be happy to welcome us."

King Bertram nodded just as Rastan burst into the room, a guard on his heels. He said, "So what am I supposed to do now?"

The guard tried to remove him, but Bertram said, "Leave him. We'll talk with him."

The guard nodded and left.

Then Bertram looked at Rastan and said, "Why, anything you want."

"But I'm not qualified for anything now that I don't have any magic," complained Rastan.

Sapphire said, "We could take your memories as well, and then you wouldn't remember that you had magic in the first place."

"No, no," said Rastan hastily. "I don't want that. I've seen Clyde and Durkin. No, I don't want that, but I'm not sure where to go or what I'm qualified to do."

Jasper looked at his father and said, "Go anywhere you like, but not to Dragonwind. We don't want you."

Rastan looked ashamed and said, "Yeah, I kinda figured that. I don't want to be anywhere around dragons anyway, after they killed my great-great-grandfather and stole our land."

Sapphire said, "Rastan, you should know that we never killed your ancestor. He actually was very close to one of our dragons, who was killed by your own people. Your ancestor couldn't bear to be without his dragon companion, so he faded away. We tried to help him, but he was too lost without his friend. And the hunters took your land, not the dragons. We did make our home in the aerie, primarily because none of the humans wanted that land, but we never have touched the lands around Dragonwind."

Rastan looked at her carefully before he said, "So you're saying my grandfather lied?"

"Maybe he didn't lie so much as believe a false story," said Sapphire.

"I don't know what I'm going to do now," said Rastan. "My entire life has been centered on getting justice for my great-great-grandfather. You say that was all a lie?"

"I'm sorry," said Sapphire.

"What do I do now? I have to start over."

"If you really want to start over," said King Bertram, "I can certainly find a place for you. But I would expect hard work. I can think of several things you could do to make the poor district in the capital a better place. It wouldn't be easy, but it would go a long way toward making up for some of your crimes."

"I'll take it," said Rastan. "What about Basil? Did you ever find him?"

King Bertram laughed and said, "I bet he's still in the dungeons."

Then Bertram called to one of his guards and asked him to find Basil. The guard returned in a few minutes carrying an unconscious Basil.

Sapphire said, "Let's wake him up, and I'll strip his magic before he can teleport." Then she looked at Rastan and said, "He'll still have his memories, though, so he'll remember you."

"But his magic will be gone?"

"Yes," said Sapphire. "He'll be in the same position as you are now. If I were you, I wouldn't pair up with him. If the two of you start any plotting, we will know."

King Bertram said, "Rastan, you may go see the captain of the guard, and he'll assign you quarters. We'll talk tomorrow."

After Rastan left the room, Bertram had a guard throw cold water on Basil, and as he spluttered awake, opening his eyes, Sapphire locked onto his glance, and in a second, his magic was gone.

Basil looked around and then said, "What did you do?"

Sapphire said, "I've taken away your magic. If you know what's good for you, you'll leave the palace quietly and never come back."

Basil looked around at the group and then headed, almost running, out of the room, followed by a guard who would be sure he left.

Everyone laughed at Basil's departure.

Then, once the laughter died down, Ty said, "Well, we'd better head back to Dragonwind. It will be nice to get some rest without having to worry about snowstorms or other disasters. I do hope things settle down for a while now."

"Hear, hear," the others said.

About the Author

Daphne Ashling Purpus has a great love of fantasy literature, cultivated during her career as a librarian and teacher. She now lives and writes on beautiful Vashon Island in the Pacific Northwest, where she tutors students of all ages at the local alternative schools, StudentLink and FamilyLink.

A prolific fiction writer, Purpus is the author of eleven fantasy novels about dragons, including *Dragon Rider; The Egg That Wouldn't Hatch; Dragon Magic; The Dragon Who Chooses Twice; The Girl, the Gryphon, and the Dragon, The Mage's Dilemma; The Seer's Challenge; The Fox, the Stag, and the Dragon; Dragon Sanctuary;* and most recently, *Dragons, Mages, and Magic.* Her poetry is published in *A Year of Haiku.*

In addition to tutoring, writing, and reading, Purpus can be found caring for her dog and four cats.

www.ingramcontent.com/pod-product-compliance
Lightning Source LLC
Chambersburg PA
CBHW060152130626
46556CB00006B/2605